Furball and the Mokes

A.N. Wilson has written over twenty stories for grown-ups, many of which have won prizes, such as the Somerset Maugham Award (for *The Healing Art*) and the 1988 Whitbread Award (for the biography *Tolstoy*). He has also written a volume of guinea-pig stories called *Hazel*, and a tale of an old cat looking back over his life, *Stray*, both of which will be published by Corvus in 2012. He has had many pets in his life, including dogs and cats. His three daughters have, between them, had rabbits, guinea-pigs, hamsters, gold-fish and dogs. This story is based on the real life of his daughter Georgie's hamster, who kept getting lost.

Furball
and the Mokes

A.N. WILSON

Illustrated by
Luisa Crosbie

CORVUS

First published in Great Britain in 2011
by Corvus, an imprint of Atlantic Books Ltd.

Copyright © A.N. Wilson, 2011
Illustrations © Luisa Crosbie, 2011

9 8 7 6 5 4 3 2 1

A CIP catalogue record for this book is available from the British Library.

ISBN: 978 1 84887 954 6 (Hardback)
ISBN: 978 0 85789 447 2 (Ebook)

Printed in Great Britain by the MPG Books Group

Corvus
An imprint of Atlantic Books Ltd
Ormond House
26-27 Boswell Street
London WC1N 3JZ

www.corvus-books.co.uk

For Georgie, with happy memories of little Chum.

CHAPTER ONE

Trouble Aloft

Chum nibbled on a cherry that the Giant had left in the cage. It was a good juicy cherry. Before the Giant had left the room, her large hand, several times larger than Chum herself, had been lowered into the cage. First, it had scattered seeds among the sawdust on the floor. Then it had added a cabbage stalk. Finally, it had put a dandelion leaf just in front of Chum's nose.

Being a hamster – which Chum was – she never knew when the next meal would be. Better safe than sorry. If in doubt, pouch it. Chum had hastily gobbled as much of the food as possible into her cheek pouches – seeds, the stalk, the leaf, the cherry. Now she was alone, and safe, she could de-pouch, and eat the food at her leisure. She started with the cherry, sitting upright on her haunches and holding the cherry in her small pink paws.

Through the bars of the cage, she could see the big room that the Giant called the kitchen.

Chum's cage was on a ledge. She could see the door to the larder where they kept most of their dry food. She could see the fridge. She could see the large dresser where they kept her bag of straw, her sawdust and her seeds.

As she ate the cherry, and stared into the middle-distance, she heard voices.

They weren't voices like the Giant's and her friends'. In fact, they weren't human voices at all.

The first voice said, 'Are they gorn ven?'

And the other said, 'The little oom-varmint said as ow she ad to go ter school.'

'School, eh – that's a larf. Ow abart the grown-ups?'

'The oom-fella – e went out a long time ago.'

'How about the oom-woman?'

'She took the varmint to school.'

'So what's it going to be then? Biscuits, anyone?'

Chum found this conversation very puzzling and very interesting. Clearly there were some creatures on the other side of the room, who had been following the movements of the Giant and her mum and dad. Chum wondered if the creatures had noticed her. She didn't wonder for long, since she heard a voice from behind her packet of seeds.

'If you're going past the furball's seeds nab a handful for Junior.'

'They feed that furball too much in stir.'

'Did you see what the brat just give 'er – a cherry – a leaf – seeds – I don't know – I really don't.'

'It doesn't seem right giving all that to a furball.'

Chum felt indignant. She realized that by 'furball' they meant herself.

'Mind you,' said one of the voices, 'I wouldn't swap er life for ours – not I. Locked in stir. Fussed over by them brats. Only let out when one of them oomans wants to squeeze er. No ooman's gonna squeeze me. You wouldn't see *me* letting myself be turned into a *pet*.'

The voice said this last word with real disgust.

Chum was just taking in what the creatures were saying about her when, out of the very top of her packet of seeds on the dresser – *her* packet – there appeared, first a sharp pink nose, then a pale grey, grubby little face, then a pair of greyish-pink little ears, and finally the whole skinny body – greyish-black, dusty and sly – of a London house mouse.

'They're dry, these seeds,' it was saying, 'too dry.'

'Chuck us down some all the same,' said another.

The first mouse spat a few seeds at another mouse who had come round the side of the dresser.

'This ain't dry,' said the second mouse.

'Only cos I spit it.'

Chum wondered if they had asked permission to eat from her seedbox and decided they had not. She was still rather angry that they had called her 'furball', and thought it was pathetic that the mice either could not, or would not *pouch* the seeds, like a well-brought-up hamster. Instead, they put seeds in their mouths and spat.

'Good old furball,' laughed the mouse at the top of Chum's seed packet. This cheeky mouse either lost its balance at this point, or it was dancing on top of Chum's packet. But – oh no! – the energetic scuttering of the mouse caused the seed packet on the dresser to fall over. Down on to the floor fell a shower of seeds, straw and sawdust.

'That's more like it,' said one mouse.

'Ta, Furball – great seeds,' laughed another.

A rain of Chum's seeds cascaded from the dresser to the kitchen floor.

'I am not,' said Chum, 'called Furball.'

She had not intended to say the words out loud. She often said things out loud to herself – it was her way of thinking. So it was a bit of a shock when she heard a high, rather menacing little voice imitating what she had just said.

'Oh! Listen to er – *Ai am not called Furball.*'

There was high excited laughter among the mice.

'You oughta get outta that cage, mate – help yourself to food – and not wait till the oomans feel like dishing up.'

'I wouldn't take no food from oomans,' said another mouse. 'Ooms kill us. They'll kill you one day, Furball.'

Chum listened with indignant astonishment. Then she said, through the bars of her cage, 'But they look after me.'

'They look *ah-fta* me…' Another imitation of her voice by the mice. It was not a very good imitation.

'They done the other furball in,' said one of the mice.

'What *other* furball – I mean, hamster?' asked Chum.

She was looking across the kitchen at the mouse who had just spoken, the one who was looking up at her. She was an agile little mouse. She scuttered across the kitchen and managed to climb up the cupboard door and on to the ledge so that her pointed little grey face was looking closely at Chum's.

The mouse peered at Chum. Always hungry, the keen, clever, little grey mouse saw how plump the hamster was. Chum was clever as hamsters go but she had never had to use her cleverness for survival. If the mouse stopped being clever for an instant she would be in danger. Yet though the mouse was grey and thin and darting, while Chum was a light sandy-brown with clean pampered fur and a snowy-white chest and well-fed body, they were both little rodents who had more in common with one another than they did with the human race – the oomans or ooms as the mice called humans.

'There was another hamster?' asked Chum.

'Before you,' said the mouse. 'Murphy, they called im. Nice old bleeder. E'd call out cheerio to us now and then – known what I mean. Sometimes warn us if there were trouble aloft.'

'Trouble aloft?' asked Chum.

'If there was ooms coming. E'd keep us *informed*

like. Tell us if they'd had pie 'n that.'

'Pie?'

The mice on the other side of the kitchen could hear the word *pie* and seven or eight of them now came from behind the dresser in hungry anticipation.

'Pie? Where's the pie?'

'Furball says there's pie.'

'Where – where –'

'Chicken pies they were. Very tasty,' said the main mouse, the one who was talking to Chum through the bars of her cage.

'Pies! Pies!' called the mice.

'We're just *talking* about a pie, *stoopid*,' said the main mouse. 'There ain't no pie.'

'But,' said Chum, 'Murphy, the other hamster…?'

It was true. She had heard the Giant talking about Murphy, and the Giant's dad sometimes called *her* – Chum! – Murphy by mistake.

'Oh,' said the mouse, 'they done Murphy in.'

'What's done him in?'

'Fixed him.'

'Fixed?' Chum knew that the mouse was talking of

something unpleasant, but she didn't understand the words. Done him in? What had they done to Murphy, the human beings? And in what had they done him?

'Killed him,' said the mouse simply.

'Dug an ole in the garden – dropped him in it, like. Threw earth over im.'

'And filled it up with earth?' Chum could not easily believe her ears. What she heard was beyond her experience. She had no knowledge of death. She had never seen a dead animal. She didn't know that she herself would die.

'Filled it up. Buried old Murph. Cleaned out iz cage. Few days later, you come. It'll be your turn next, my friend. They've probably dug the ole fer yer already.'

'Are you *sure*?'

But as Chum asked the question, the mouse froze. They could hear the noise of a front door opening. The chief mouse called to the others, '*Scarper.*'

Chum watched with admiration as the little group of mice disappeared under the dresser. Some of them squeezed through the quite tiny crevices between the top of the skirting board and the wall.

'I'm Moke – Mokey Moke,' said the chief mouse as she left Chum.

'I'm Chum,' was what she wanted to say but she found herself silent. Chum was what *they* called her – the ooms, the ones who had buried the last hamster in the garden. How could he breathe, with all that earth on top of him? She liked to *burrow* herself. She liked making her way through the plastic tubes that the Giant had put in her cage to amuse her and exercise her. And she liked playing with the straw and newspaper and making tunnels for herself beneath them. But to be *buried* – in heavy, damp, garden mud – was horrible, really horrible. Could it be *true*?

She watched Mokey scutter head first down the cupboard door and disappear.

A few minutes later, the giant's dad entered. He turned on the music box in the corner and clattered for a long time – first lowering plates and pans into some soapy water, then taking the cloth things which giants wear over their bodies, placing them on a narrow table and rubbing them up and down with a hot shiny thing which made a steamy, clothy smell. After a while, a long while, the Giant's dad found a little brush and swept up the seeds on the floor – but not every single one. For, when he had touched the music box and stopped the sound, and left the room, Chum heard a scuttling, scuttering sound under the cupboard. And out came Mokey Moke – quick as a flash. She ran across the floor, grabbed the few remaining seeds in her mouth and turned.

'Watcha, Furb!' she squeaked before disappearing behind the dresser.

CHAPTER TWO

Mouse Droppings
Everywhere

Kitty's mum shouted from the larder. 'I don't *believe* it!'

'What?' asked Dad.

He knew what the answer would be. For several weeks now, he had been sweeping the larder with a small dustpan and brush whenever he found half-chewed bits of paper, crumbs or mouse droppings. He did so because he was lazy and didn't want all the trouble which would follow when Alex, Kitty's mum, discovered they had mice in the larder. The last time this had happened, they'd had to remove from the shelves every cardboard cereal carton, every packet of biscuits, every box of pasta – in short, anything through which the mice could nibble with their sharp little teeth.

'There are mouse droppings *everywhere*,' called Kitty's mum. 'Oh, *no*! And they've eaten through the bottom of –'

Kitty and her dad heard Mum's reaction as she lifted a packet of Rice Crispies and found that mice had chewed a hole in the bottom. Rice Crispies were pouring out on to the larder floor.

Kitty said, 'I told you it might be mice that had knocked over Chum's food bag last week.'

'And there we were,' said Dad, 'blaming you for spilling food on the floor.'

Mum, who had by now finished sweeping up Rice Crispies and mouse droppings, came into the kitchen.

'I can't bear it,' she said. 'It took such *ages* to get rid of them last time.'

'I just don't know how they could get in,' said Dad. 'Do you suppose they live outside the house and come in when it's raining?'

'Mum, is it all right if I take a bit of carrot from the fridge and give it to Chum?' interrupted Kitty.

She was eleven and lived alone with her houseproud mother and father. Except Dad wasn't quite as tidy as Kitty and her mum. Being neat is a gift – and they had it.

'We must be especially careful,' said Mum, 'not to leave out any food which might attract them.'

'They couldn't get into Chum's cage, could they?' asked Kitty.

'I shouldn't think so,' said Dad.

'Let's hope you're right,' said Mum, 'and they've just come in from the garden to escape last night's rain. Maybe they won't come again.'

Kitty's dad was silent, concealing the fact that for weeks he had seen the telltale signs of mice.

'It's funny in a way,' said Mum. 'We keep one little rodent as a pet, and then spend so much energy driving away these other little rodents.'

Kitty put on her 'Chum' voice and pretended to speak for her hamster.

'Allie – I am *not* one little rodent.'

'Yes, you *are*,' said Mum, whose name was Alex, leaning over Chum's cage and looking into her curranty little eyes. When Kitty pretended to be Chum, Mum was Allie and Dad was 'Mister Peter'.

'I am not just a little rodent,' squeaked Kitty in her Chum voice. 'I'm not, I'm not.'

'Oh, look, it's rather sweet,' said Dad, 'Chum's sitting up and doing her impression of a meerkat.'

Chum was the second hamster they had bought. The first, a much slower and in some ways statelier fellow, had been called Murphy. When, after something over a year, he died, Kitty and Mum had decided to replace him at once. They had returned from the pet shop with the tiny, hyper-energetic, fudge-and-white coloured Chum only days after Murphy's sad funeral in the garden. All three of them had quickly grown to like, and then actually to love, the tiny Chum.

As well as being a fast runner, Chum had a bright sunny outlook on life. When not asleep inside the cashmere sock which Dad provided for her bedding, she was eagerly looking out at the world. When out of her cage, she sometimes became what Kitty called 'hyper', running round and round the room. Kitty and her mum believed that Chum both needed, and enjoyed, this form of exercise. Dad, more timorous, was everlastingly afraid that she would get lost or run away.

CHAPTER THREE

Free as the Mokes

'Wotcha, Furba.'

Chum stirred a little in the comfort of the cashmere sock. Her eyes were still closed. Her fur and her eyelids were flecked with sawdust.

The voice in her ear persisted. 'Ope don't mind, Furba. Elped erself ter seeds. Good.'

Mokey Moke had not asked if she could eat Chum's seeds. But it made a change that she had apologised – or sort of apologised – for eating them.

'Ad carrot too – ope don't mind, Furba, ole mucka.'

Chum opened her eyes and saw Mokey's eager little grey face close to hers. Mokey Moke gave off a strong smell. But Chum didn't mind this.

The first time she had seen the mice in the kitchen, dancing on her food packet and making a riot, she had felt angry. She felt they were stealing *her* food, making a mess in *her* kitchen. But after they had scuttled behind the dresser and life was quiet again, she found that she missed the mice. There had been several conversations with them since then. In fact, the mice came each evening. The younger ones were still cheeky – and silly too. A couple of them bit a hole in a bag of flour in the food cupboard and rolled about in it. Then they had a game which was like the kind of game Chum had watched the Giant and her friends have when the world became very cold one day and was covered with thick white stuff they called snow. The Giant and her friends had thrown *their* white stuff at one another just as the young mice were now prancing in the flour, which spread from the cupboard shelves to the kitchen floor.

'Said I'd come,' said Mokey Moke.

Chum yawned and began to take in the strangeness of the situation.

'Mokey,' she said, 'Good morning, good evening – whatever time it is. What – what are you doing in my cage?'

'Said I'd get. Said I'd get yer. Said I'd get yer outta stir.'

Chum looked about her cage. It was quite a roomy cage, made from plastic-lined metal wire. It had an upper and a lower storey, but, to add variety to life and to give her the chance to exercise, there was a system of transparent plastic tubes, which ran both inside and outside the cage. To make them easier to clean, these tubes were made in detachable segments held together by bright blue and orange rings.

Once a week or so the Giant would clean these tubes and give Chum new straw, sawdust and newspaper on her cage floor. Sometimes, when the Giant was away, it was left to the grown-ups to put the tubes back together. This must have happened now. The Giant had gone for a sleepover with her friends and Dad had attempted the complicated puzzle of putting the tubes back together. Clearly one of the rings hadn't been connected properly. The tubing had collapsed and the resourceful mouse Mokey Moke had crept through the gaping hole. Mokey Moke nuzzled against Chum's side and repeated, 'Wotcha.'

Chum looked at her tube. Instead of being an enclosed transparent tunnel through which she could run down to the basement floor of the cage, up a side, through the dining area, down to the basement, and up the side over and over again, the tube was now an open window.

'You're free, Furba, ole girl. Free as the mokes.'

Chum looked at Mokey Moke and, for a moment, she said nothing. Then she put one cautious pink paw forward, then another. She walked slowly towards the hole. The young mice playing in the flour on the other side of the kitchen paused to look up at her. Two older mice who were standing beside the gap in the skirting board were also staring up at the cage. Chum stepped out through the hole, followed by Mokey Moke. The mice in the kitchen gave a big cheer.

'Furb. Good on yer, Furball!'

The squeaks and whistles had much of the old mockery. Chum was beginning to get used to this.

Even when speaking or squeaking to one another the mice mocked and teased. It was their way of speaking. But they were genuinely pleased and friendly as they welcomed her into the kitchen.

The first time she had seen them in that room – a few weeks ago – Chum had felt indignation that these invaders were in *her* kitchen, eating *her* seeds. She didn't feel like that any more. She had stopped thinking that the kitchen or the seeds or indeed anything, except perhaps the comfortable cashmere sock, exactly *belonged* to her. At first, the mice had scared her and annoyed her. They still did a little bit, but much less than they had done at first. Now she had come to like Mokey Moke and the antics of the younger mice – yes, they could be annoying, but they were also funny.

With pink claws attached to the outside of the cage, Chum climbed down and scuttled across the kitchen to the mice beside the dresser.

'You'll byable to store it good,' said one of the mice by the skirting board.

'Thank you,' said Chum – she was sure that he had meant a compliment since his sentence ended with the word '*good*' – but she hadn't quite understood the rest.

'Well then,' said Mokey Moke, 'let's set to – sumin yer appy, Furba?'

'Oh, very,' said Chum.

'*Git on wivvit ven*,' said the second of the two mice beside the skirting board. '*Parck.*'

'Parck?' She was puzzled.

'That fing wot you do with your marfy,' said Mokey Moke.

'I don't do anything with my marfy – in fact I don't know what marfy is.'

Mokey Moke put a seed in her mouth and did a rather bad imitation of a hamster pouching food in her cheeks.

'You want me to pouch food for you? Marfy means mouth?'

'Comprenny at larsto – plarsto,' said one of the mice by the skirting board. They scampered forward to a piece of bread which had either fallen or been dragged by them to the kitchen floor.

'If yer woody,' said Mokey Moke politely.

'If I would – chew and pouch?'

'And liver arpliss.'

'Deliver to your place.'

She was beginning to twig. 'Where exactly?'

'If you'd park a load I'll show yer, Furba, ole girl,' said the mouse by the skirting board. Chum later learned his name was Nobby, and his brother was Buster.

Chum advanced towards the hunk of bread and set to. The mice were evidently impressed by the speed with which she managed to store so much bread in her cheek pouches. Soon her hamster-head and neck and even her shoulders had changed shape, and she resembled (as the Giant had once said) a hammer-headed shark.

'Ready, Furball-mite?'

Chum nodded.

'Good on yer.'

Mokey Moke ran – almost danced – under the dresser and Chum followed. Here the gap between the skirting board was even wider. Mokey Moke managed to squeeze through this gap quite easily. For Chum, it was a bit of a challenge, but she did it.

She dropped down in the darkness.

'Yer could leave it ere and go back fer more?' asked Mokey Moke.

Glad to help her new friends, Chum de-pouched the bread, or nearly all of it, keeping back a little in her pouch. In case. You never knew.

'Ven if you was ter. Ever so much obleege-oh!' said Mokey Moke, with one of her strange squeaky laughs.

Chum had landed on a soft, dark, dusty patch of flour. She could only dimly make out the hole at the top of the skirting board. She tried to climb towards it, but at the first attempt she only slithered to the ground again. Not to be outdone by a mouse, she made another attempt, and by great effort she was able to hold on to a brick surface with her claws and clamber towards the gap. Getting back into the kitchen was harder than it had been to get out. But she managed it and was soon munching at the hunk of loaf on the floor, filling her pouch once more. It was satisfying to hear the mice below admiring how she did it.

'Cor – see how fast she done that? Cor – ow she

done that? Cor – see that? Vanished like magic that did.'

She made three difficult journeys to and fro, and in quite a short time she had shifted more bread than a mouse could have carried in ten journeys. It was when she was sitting on the kitchen floor and filling her pouch for a fourth time that two of the younger mice began to shout. 'Ooms! Ooms!'

They heard a door open, footsteps on the stairs. The mice scampered under the dresser and Chum followed. By the time human feet had appeared in the kitchen, two of the leaner mice had scuttered with the greatest of ease behind the skirting board.

From where she hovered under the dresser, Chum could see the Giant's school shoes. She could hear a tap being turned as the Giant helped herself to a glass of water.

Then the Giant called out loudly, 'Mum – have you seen Chum's cage?'

Another pair of shoes came into the kitchen: Mum's stylish olive-green Converse.

'C'mon, Furb – come *on*,' urged Mokey Moke.

Chum hesitated a moment. A bit of her wanted to run out to the Giant. Probably the Giant would pick her up and stroke her; possibly she would give her a piece of parsley or half a cherry. But another part of Chum caught the panic felt by the mokes. It was not, quite, that she saw the Giant and her mum as enemies – as Mokey and the other mice did. But she felt the fear of the mokes. When Mokey Moke ran, Chum ran. Mokey Moke scuttered up the wall; Chum followed. Once more she squeezed through that tight gap at the top of the skirting board. This time, rather than sitting down at once and de-pouching two cheeks full of bread, she followed Mokey Moke who was running, running, running through long tunnels into deeper and deeper blackness.

CHAPTER FOUR

A Terrible Emptiness

Kitty was trying not to cry, and trying not to be furious. Four hours had now passed since she came back from school. The previous night she had been for a sleepover with a friend. She had left her mum and dad with the very simple task of looking after one small hamster in a cage. She had not asked them to take a dog for a walk, or exercise a monkey or go swimming with a dolphin. Just look after one hamster. And what had they done? They had somehow not noticed that the plastic tubing at the side of Chum's cage had come to bits. Someone (Kitty refused to believe it was herself – she suspected her dad), *someone* had been *stupid* enough not to fix the plastic rings tightly. She had once caught her dad, when he was meant to be helping her clean out Chum's cage, putting the tubes back together in such a way that the hamster could not get from the top floor of her cage to the sock bed at the bottom without jumping half a metre or clambering down the side of the cage.

Kitty had only had Chum a few months but already she loved her very much. In fact all three of them loved Chum – Dad, Mum and Kitty – which was why they all felt so very sad without her.

Kitty sat on the sofa watching TV, but not really paying any attention to what was happening on the screen. Mum, who had put a few pieces of Chum's favourite cheese near a hole at the bottom of the stairs, had said there was no point in searching. The animal could be *anywhere*. Dad was lying on the floor beside the cooker. He thought she might be there. He was holding out a bit of carrot and calling 'Chum! Chum!' in piteous tones.

Kitty knew it was by accident that Chum had got lost, but she couldn't help being angry with both her father and her mother.

'She'll come back when she's hungry,' said Mum.

'Unless she meets a rat,' said Dad.

'We don't have rats,' said Mum.

'There might be rats – where she's gone,' said Dad.

'And where's that, I'd like to know.'

Kitty, silent, thought, *they have lost my hamster. Now they are going to embarrass me by having a quarrel.*

But they held back – just – from a row. This didn't stop Dad from talking about it all in a way that was both annoying and alarming. He was only thinking aloud, but he sounded like a teacher – telling them things they knew already.

'Chum wasn't born in the wild,' he said. 'She was born in a pet shop. All hamsters in the Western world descend from one pair that bred in captivity in the year 1930. I know we have all sorts of jokes and fantasies about Chum coming from Syria, and knowing about life in the desert. The truth is, though, she was born in captivity. She's learned absolutely no survival skills. She was fed by her mother in a cage. Then she was fed by the pet-shop people. Then we bought her. Apart from the rare occasions when we let her out for a run on the carpet, she has never been anywhere, never had to forage for her own food, never had to find her own water to drink. Even if she doesn't meet a rat, it's hard to think she stands much chance of surviving—'

'Thanks, Dad!' Kitty had by now heard more than she could bear. 'It's bad enough Chum going missing – without you spelling out what's so *obvious*!' And she stormed out of the room, slamming the door.

'Kitty – I didn't mean…'

She was half aware of her dad's voice, saying he was sorry.

A bit later – maybe a lot later – she could hear her mum and dad outside her bedroom door.

'She'll be OK. Leave her. She needs some space.'

Were Mum and Dad talking about her, or her hamster?

'I wasn't fussing.'

'She needs to be alone for a bit.'

Later still, Mum – by now in her pyjamas – came into Kitty's bedroom. Normally, Kitty would bring Chum upstairs with her. While she lay in bed, drifting off to sleep, she would be comforted by the sound of the small animal moving about in her cage. Tonight, the room seemed horribly silent. Outside, in the London night, cars and buses passed by, trains rumbled. Inside, there was only a bleak silence, a terrible emptiness.

'Come on, Kitty. Come on, Stinker.' Mum wasn't being rude – it was a joke name she sometimes used. Kitty sat up in bed and let Mum hug her. Blearily – for it was late – she went to the bathroom, put on pyjamas, cleaned her teeth. Tomorrow was another school day. Mum had reminded her of this, and into Kitty's mind came the comforting thought of her friends. She thought of lessons she had not prepared for. She thought of the netball game they would play in the afternoon. But every now and then, like a stab of toothache returning, she would remember the empty cage downstairs and wonder whether Chum was alive or dead.

CHAPTER FIVE

The Edge of Lundine

Chum, or Furball as she now half-thought of herself, ran faster than the mokes. She ran and ran. Sometimes the going underfoot was made of fluff and dust and it was a bit like running first through soft sand, then through feathers. Then it became much rougher – loose stones, rubble, hunks of brick and plaster much bigger than herself to be climbed or avoided. Because it was so dark, she couldn't make out a path. She simply charged ahead.

'Cor – you're some runner, Furball, ole matey,' called Mokey Moke from behind.

It seemed the right moment to pause.

Chum was very glad that she hadn't de-pouched

the final load before the mice sounded the alarm in the kitchen. She de-pouched now, and Mokey, Buster and Nobby shared the feast of crumbs and seeds.

'Close one,' said Nobby.

'Reckon you're safe wiv us, eh, Furba?' said Buster.

Furball, as she was now in the process of thinking herself, had never felt less safe in her life, but she felt very excited.

The mokes, talking with their mouths full, exclaimed about the excellence of the provisions.

'Vese seeds from your pocket ven.'

'Luvva nice bitta bread.'

Chum called the chief mouse, her special friend, Mokey Moke, just as they called her Furb, Furba or sometimes Furball. But she was beginning to realise that all the mice called themselves mokes.

While they stopped to get their breath back and eat Chum's food supplies, the mokes told her more about the world outside her cage.

The mokes called their world Lundine – at least that was the name of the house where they lived, and the spaces just beside it. They explained it was made up of endless tunnels, holes, puddles, burrows and dark places. Its chief inhabitants were the mokes, of course, but there were also narks (who were to be dreaded). The narks, whith their big teeth and long thick tails – called rats by the ooms – were the mokes' chief enemies in Lundine itself. They told Chum: if you hear or – worse still – if you see a nark, scarper. That's the only thing for it. Just run. You'll never be able to fight a nark, and you'll never be able to outwit him.

Chum shivered when she heard that outside Lundine there were hundreds of enemies – it was all enemies. There were the snarks, who were like narks, only their tails were grey and bushy not pink and moist. They lived in the trees but they'd fight mokes for their food. So would most fevvas – the bigger fevvas that the ooms called pigeons, gulls, starlings. Even the little fevvas (sparrers, robins and such) wanted watching. 'And,' one of them added, 'then there are the real killers, the snarls, what ooms call their little friends the doggies, and the claws what ooms call cats.'

There were hundreds of moke stories – the ones their parents had told them and the scary ones they told each other as they huddled in their makeshift dusty nests under floorboards and stairs, about snarls and claws. Claws were the worst of the two, of course. They'd wait hours to catch a moke. 'And when a claws has caught you it won't just kill outright, like a snarl might,' they said. 'Not claws. He'll play with you and worrit you and hold you pincered and kebabbed on his claws, he will.'

But the mokes told Chum there was a funny thing about snarls and claws. They're not just doing it for themselves. They are working for the ooms. It's the ooms who control the whole world inside and outside Lundine – that bright, noisy, cold, often wet world outdoors away from the shadows where the mokes felt safest. As far as the mokes could tell, the ooms devoted their entire existence to fighting, killing, exterminating mokes, and they enlisted every friend they could. Mokey Moke had heard it said the ooms could make the fevvas catch mokes for them, and though she'd never seen it done, she could believe it. Ooms did not eat mokes – at least she didn't think they ate them – not like claws or snarls will eat a moke. It seemed as though

they just wanted to kill mokes for the fun of it. Ooms –
they were like the claws, only worse. It was just killing,
not eating, that ooms liked.

Furball didn't learn all this at once. She picked it
up little by little, chiefly from Mokey Moke, but also
from the other mokes. Sometimes – as when they told
her what the claws like to do if they catch a fevva or
a moke – it was a long explanation. Mostly, though,
Furball picked it all up from odd remarks made by one
or other of the mokes.

'Good bread this, Furball ole girl,' Nobby, one of
the young mokes, had said between mouthfuls. 'You
don't always know with food what's on the floor.'

'But there's usually food on the floor of my cage.'

'My case rests,' said Nobby with a strange laugh.

What did he mean? His case rests? What case? The
Giant had several huge boxes with handles which she
called shoot cases. And there was a thing into which she
stuffed her drawing things, and a bit of rubber – pencil
case it was. But the case rests? Mysterious.

Nobby's special mate, his brother Buster, explained
it later.

'It's the ooms,' he said. 'Like Old Uncle Barney and his kids. The ooms put *stuff* on it, know whadd-eye mean?'

'No,' said Furball.

'*Stuff*,' laughed Buster. 'Finish yer. Kaput. End. Curtains. Finito.'

'Like when they put Murf in the garden earth?' asked Furball.

'They put it on yer food.' Buster never answered a direct question. 'They put it on yer food to get rid of yer. It's one way.'

'Another's the old snapper,' said Nobby. 'Aunty Flo went the snapper way. Remember Aunty Flo? Chattering to us bout this cheese she'd seen – right – on the oom-floor. Cheese. Loved a bit of cheese, Aunty Flo did. Got all excited. Offered us kids a nibble. Run out to get it.'

'She got it all right,' said Buster.

'Splat,' said Nobby.

'All in all I'd rather have floor-food than the old snapper,' said Buster.

Furball did not want either. She was silent. Was

it possible that the mokes were simply wrong? Could it be that the various accidents which they described were simply that – accidents? Or were the ooms – all the ooms – even the Giant, whose warm hands had so often enclosed Furball's furry little body (when she'd been Chum), even the Giant's mum and dad, killing other animals, one after another?

Furball had always felt safe in her cage, and safe with the Giant. The ooms had given her plentiful, various foods to enjoy – fruits and vegetables, as well as fresh water. Running away had been an adventure, but it had not felt safe – the opposite. And now she was very confused.

If the mokes had the right way of looking at things, then the ooms only wanted to keep a hamster so that, one day, a day of their choosing, they would bury her in mud. Furball still wasn't sure what killing meant, but she could not forget what one of the mokes had described to her – the ooms standing round in the garden putting old Murf in the ground, and water coming out of their eyes like the time that the Giant's dad chopped up onions and dropped a *lot* on the floor.

Now that wasn't floor-food and no one died eating that and it really was delicious.

Furball and the mokes had come to a long, low dusty tunnel at the end of which, very faintly, light could be seen. The further they walked towards the light, the wetter became the ground underfoot. In fact the fluff and dust soon became mud. Some of the mokes licked it, but Furball didn't like to do this – it was so very dirty!

'We're coming to where Lundine stops,' Mokey Moke told her. 'Out there – well, yer on yer own out there, all right. Out there's fevvas – there's a claw what sits on the wall trying to catch the fevvas, there's snarks and there's narks. And that's why, Furba, me ole mate, most mokes never leave Lundine. That Out There – it's a jungle, that.'

Furball did not doubt Mokey Moke's words but, now they had come this far, she wanted to explore. So she edged her way forward towards the hole. The nearer she got, the dirtier she became, and she would dearly have liked to pause and have a good wash. But Mokey Moke and one or two of the other mokes were behind her. So she tiptoed as fast and as delicately as she could towards the hole.

It felt good to put her nose through the hole and to sniff the good, fresh air beyond it. Furball pushed her nose further until her whole head had emerged from the hole in the brickwork. She was in the backyard of the house. On the green, slimy paving stones there were some huge watering cans. High, high above the watering cans was a tube with a lid on top of it. The Giant's mum had hung it on a hook on the brick wall and it was half full of… seeds. A number of birds – coal tits and siskins – were clustered round this object, and as they pecked at the seeds which came out into a small tray at the bottom of the tube, many of the seeds fell down into the paved yard. In fact the birds were pecking so vigorously that they were knocking down almost as many seeds as they pecked into their beaks. It was as if it were raining seeds from the sky.

'Watch yerself,' Mokey Moke warned her. 'You don't wanna go out there on yer own, girly.'

But Furball did. She wanted to go out there very much indeed. She wanted to pouch seeds, and this desire made her deaf to Mokey Moke's warnings, and blind to all the dangers which would face a small hamster running out into a yard where these other creatures – the creatures the ooms called magpies, squirrels and rats – were living. They were creatures who were also hungry for seeds and they would fight and even kill for them.

'Seeds,' said Furball excitedly. 'Seeds. Seeds. Seeds.'

'Watch it, Furball,' said Mokey Moke. 'Careful, my girl.'

'Seeds,' gasped Furball, and she scuttled out into the yard.

CHAPTER SIX

Kitty's Daydream

'And what words show us that Billy was frightened?' asked Mrs Atkins.

Some of the girls in the class giggled. They weren't laughing because of what their teacher had said, but because she had the strange habit of scratching between her legs when she asked questions. She didn't seem to know she was doing it. Normally, Kitty would have been giggling at the teacher too, but today her thoughts were elsewhere. The thought of the missing hamster gnawed at her heart. It was almost an actual physical pain, a numb pain in her chest.

After the death of her first hamster, Murphy, Kitty felt a sharp sorrow that was like a grazed knee. It stung.

But Mum and she had agreed that if Murphy died they would buy another hamster at once. So they had done. It didn't stop her missing Murphy. But it made the pain much better. And in time, the pain went away.

It was Mum's jokey idea to name the new hamster 'Murphy's Dumb Chum', or Chum for short. Everyone had loved Murphy, of course they had, and there had been tears at his garden funeral. But from the start, there had been something very special about Chum. She seemed to have a stronger personality. Her black curranty eyes were not just intelligent; they were friendly. They seemed to smile. She was so quick, so energetic. She was fun.

The school lessons went on around Kitty. Mrs Atkins called what she taught 'comprehension'. Chloe, a girl in glasses who was smaller than the others in the class, had her hand up, to show that she had spotted the words in the (incredibly boring) set passage which showed that a boy named Billy was frightened.

'Chloe?' asked Mrs Atkins brightly, showing a row of rather yellow teeth.

'*He trembled*,' said Chloe. 'It's where it says, *He trembled...*'

'Good,' said Mrs Atkins. 'Anyone else? Freddie?'

'Is it where it says there was a big bang outside the window?' asked Freddie hesitantly.

'Quiet, everyone,' said Mrs Atkins, scratching between her legs with the energy of a flea-ridden chimpanzee. About six girls were giggling, partly because Freddie had given a wrong answer and partly because he had turned bright red.

'The loud noise is one of the things which *made* Billy frightened,' said Mrs Atkins. 'But what are the words which show us he *was* frightened?'

Chloe's arm had gone up again. It looked as if she hoped, with enough stretching and straining, she could reach the ceiling of the classroom.

'Maybe someone else,' said Mrs Atkins, still scratching away. Her voice had taken on the cooing tone some grown-ups adopted to address a really young child or perhaps a kitten. Everyone in the class was eleven, but she spoke as if they were six.

'What other words show he was frightened? Kitty?'

Kitty was in a daydream. She was remembering the

way she held Chum under her jumper. She remembered the feel of those little paws against her stomach, and the warmth of the little fur ball as it snuggled against her. Kitty didn't want to cry in front of the rest of the class. But when she thought of Chum, missing, perhaps stuck in a mouse hole, perhaps being mauled by a cat, it was very hard to stop her eyes filling with tears.

'Any frightened words?' said Mrs Atkins. *Scratch, scratch.*

Kitty was silent.

'I hope you are paying attention, Kitty,' said Mrs Atkins sharply. 'OK then, Chloe, another frightened word –'

'Like when it says *He trembled...*' said Chloe.

'You've already said that,' someone shouted as the whole class laughed.

'*He trembled but not just from cold,*' was what Chloe was saying, but by then there was too much noise going on for anyone to hear her.

CHAPTER SEVEN

A Bullying Snark

As she came nearer to the shower of seeds, which fell so temptingly on to the paving of the backyard, Furball could see what had happened. An enormous animal, several times larger than herself, had managed to climb the wall and with its sharp teeth had bored a hole, also larger than herself, in the plastic tube which contained the seeds. A cluster of three green finches were taking advantage of the situation and had driven away the tits. But even as these birds pecked frantically, the animal came back. It had a big, grey bushy tail and a grey furry body. It was what ooms called a squirrel and Furball's friends the mokes called a snark.

It made an aggressive hissing sound and jumped

towards the bright green birds so that they flew away. Then it continued destroying the plastic tub. As it bit, more seeds rained down into the yard beneath.

Furball's nose was raised tremblingly in the air. Her whiskers quivered expectantly. To say she was brave might be true. But it would perhaps be truer to say that she was torn between two enormously strong desires. One was the need to protect herself. The other was the need to get to those seeds, to fill her pouch with seeds, to eat seeds – seeds, seeds, seeds. In that moment it did not matter that she would have to do battle with a snark several times larger than she was herself, if she was to have even the smallest hope of a pouchful of seeds. The hunger, the need for seeds was so strong that her pink paws had scuttled towards the patch of birdseed in the yard by the back door long before she'd had the chance to think the matter over or decide whether it was safe. And the seeds were delicious. Mainly sunflowers but a few – *mmm, mmm* – she hadn't – *mm, mmm*, oh they were so good! – a few she hadn't tasted before. She had managed to fill her pouches almost to bursting before the very great danger of her situation became clear.

'Mine – *my seeds* – *mine!*' said the snark in truly threatening tones. 'Drop – drop *my seeds* – vermin!'

Chum's currant eyes met the much larger eyes of the snark. From the ledge above their heads the finches were calling out, 'Ours, ours, all seed ours,' and the starlings were imitating, 'Ours, ours', and here and there were robins, blackbirds and pigeons – all the fevvas, in short – shouting, 'Squirrels! Thieving squirrels, taking our food – ours – ours.' And another fevva would call back, 'See that little brown ball of fluff – yes, there, there, ball of fluff – *it* thinks *it* can eat our seeds now.'

'Ours – ours – ours.'

'Ball o' fluff – ball o' fluff.'

'At least squirrel'll tear its horn'd eyes out.'

'Eyes out, eyes out,' laughed the fevvas.

Chum now saw what Mokey Moke had meant when warning her about the world outside Lundine. It was truly frightening. The fevvas were singing what amounted to a chorus calling for her blood. And the great grey snark had puffed up its huge fluffy tail and bared its enormous front teeth and was about to jump on her with its claws.

Chum knew she would have no chance of winning a fight against the snark.

'Drop those seeds now,' warned the snark. But it had a particularly menacing way of speaking which meant that the words got repeated, 'Drop, drop those seeds, seeds, seeds – now, now *now*.'

The taste of the sunflower seeds was drifting from her pouches into her mouth. It was the best pouchful she'd ever had and she was not inclined to give it up for a bullying snark. On the other hand, the snark was clearly prepared, if necessary, to greedily tear the seeds out of her, as if the seeds were sweets and her pouches, and indeed her head, no more than wrapping.

'Seeds, seeds, seeds,' repeated the snark. And then it jumped.

Chum could see its front claws and its savage teeth and its angry eyes as the snark threw itself towards her with a bloodcurdling leap. It was so frightening that it made Chum freeze to the spot, and this is what saved her. The snark had leaped too far, expecting Chum to run a little way ahead. This – just – gave Chum the chance to turn and run, as fast as her short legs and pink feet would carry her, in the opposite direction.

The squirrel could leap and jump but it was a stupid animal, a fact upon which the younger finches, laughing above his head, were not slow to comment.

'Missed the fluff!,' they laughed, 'missed the fluff' This gave the fluff (Chum *just* had time to feel some indignation at this nickname) a chance to scuttle several metres across the backyard. By the time the squirrel had realised his mistake, Chum had a head start. She ran fast, away from the house and towards the small wooden garden shed where the ooms kept a few tools and a couple of deckchairs. It wasn't a large garden – only about ten metres in length. Chum had run to the end of it in a minute. Only when she reached the shed, however, did she begin to realise what she had done.

She had crossed into the great world outside Lundine. She had come into that frightening place which the mokes had told her of – the world of snarls and claws. She had left behind the house, the Giant, and all her security.

CHAPTER EIGHT

Sticky Traps

'I think we should just buy another hamster,' Dad was saying.

And Mum was saying – as if Kitty wasn't even in the room, or as if she were a little kid who could not understand what grown-ups were talking about – 'It would be a relief not having to clean out her cage every week. Maybe we should have a rest from hamsters for a while.'

'Or there's always the possibility of a D.O.G.,' said Dad.

'Dad!' said Kitty. 'I can spell *dog*, you know! I am *eleven*.'

'If we had a dog,' Mum said, 'it might deal with the

mouse problem. Have you seen the larder this morning? One of you left a packet of biscuits on the shelf…'

'It wasn't me, Mum,' said Kitty.

'Don't look at me,' said Dad.

'And they've eaten their way through the corner. There are little shreds of paper all over the larder floor, and crumbs and mouse droppings –'

'How do you know they're mouse droppings?' Dad asked.

'Oh, don't be so *annoying*,' said Mum. 'And the *smell*. We must do something to get rid of them. If they keep on bothering us, I'm going to buy sticky-traps. Mum often discussed such problems as mouse – or moth – infestations with their neighbours. 'Alan and Rupert say sticky-traps are the only way.'

'They are so cruel,' said Kitty. 'The mouse gets its feet stuck on the trap. It can't run away. It can't move. It's just *trapped* there.'

'That's the idea,' said Mum grimly.

'You could scarcely put one of those things down while C.H.U.M. was still at large.'

'*Dad*,' said Kitty, 'I can S.P.E.L.L. – right?'

CHAPTER NINE

Must Have Food!

The garden shed was warm and dry. It was an ideal place for a hamster – or for mice. You could scuttle, if you were a hamster, round and round an area which was broad and wide. It was much, much bigger than Furball's cage. Or 'stir' as the mokes called it. And in this place, she thought of herself as Furball. She did not think of herself as having a name given to her by the ooms. This was a place where a hamster could be herself. She could run about. She could hide in the dust and fluff balls behind the stacked chairs and garden tools. The mokes would love it, of that she was convinced. She could imagine her friends Nobby and Buster dancing about on top of the pile of flowerpots, or playing hide-and-seek beneath them. There would be no need to run away from the ooms on this great floor space because – well – there *were* no ooms here. It had a safe feeling to it.

Furball formed her ideas quickly – just as she ate quickly and ran quickly. She sat in the middle of the garden shed. The ideas came to her as she washed herself, licking her pink paws and rubbing behind her ears. This shed would be the ideal home for herself and the mokes. They would run away from Lundine and the ooms. They could live their own lives, free from danger. Every now and then they would have to hide – when the Giant put out food for them, for example. But for the rest of the time, they could lead their own lives, free from oom interference, free from worry, free from danger.

Now that Furball had this wonderful idea she could hardly wait to return to Lundine to tell her plan to Mokey Moke. When she had told her friend about the shed and the freedom it would give them, only one difficulty was to be faced: how to organise all the mokes into one obedient party; and how to persuade them to make the dangerous journey from the hole in Lundine wall, across the wet paving stones of the yard, past the fevvas, and the claws – and past the snark. But Furball was an optimist. The journey across the yard might be dangerous. But once she and the mokes had made the journey, and avoided the snark, the claws, the snarl and the fevvas, they would be safe inside their shed forever and ever, and the only oom they need ever see again would be the Giant when she brought them their food.

Furball squeezed under the door of the shed so that, once again, she was out in the yard. She raised her nose in the air and her whiskers twitched nervously. She looked this way and that. The snark was scampering along the lower branch of the horse chestnut tree which overhung the brick garden wall. The claws had abandoned his seat there and was prowling about at the other end of the yard, looking hungrily at the small brown fevvas that Buster called sparrers.

Furball thought that she might – just *might* – get away with it if she ran back across the yard in the direction of Lundine. But although Furball was a rash little thing, and although she did not have a wide experience of life, she was not stupid. She was not going to take any unnecessary risks. Seeing the claws, with its sharp eyes focused on the brown fevvas, was a good reminder (if Furball needed reminding) that the whole backyard, and perhaps the whole of what ooms called Nature, is based on the idea of one creature trying to catch, and eat, another creature. The claws waited to catch the fevvas. The snarl chased the claws. The big fevvas fought off the little fevvas and grabbed their seeds. The fevvas ate the worms and the flies. No doubt the big flies ate the little flies. Only the ooms (if Buster and Nobby were right) killed creatures not to eat them but just for the fun of it. *Could* this be true – of the Giant and of the Giant's mum and dad?

Furball stood there quivering at the hole in the bottom of the shed door, and looking at a hostile world. Why did they all want to fight and kill one another? It was a complete mystery to her. Surely there would always be someone to feed them if they were patient? She had the Giant to feed *her* – but weren't there Giants to feed the snarls, snarks and claws? The Giant's mum fed the fevvas. Other ooms fed the claws and the snarls.

Buster and Nobby had told her that, for mokes and other animals, it wasn't like that. They had no Giants. They had to fend for themselves. Furball thought this must be some kind of mistake. She thought that somehow, long ago, perhaps in a past which the mokes could not remember, a Giant had looked after them and fed them. Only, somehow, they had been separated from their Giant, or lost her, and that was why they had this idea of having to feed themselves. Or so Furball believed. It pleased her to find such a simple solution. In the shed, she and the mokes would be free. But of course there would always be a Giant. It never occurred to Furball that the Giant would not be there to feed her. She was sure that in the lovely new shed, she and the mokes could live in freedom but they would all be fed by the Giant.

All these muddled thoughts and ambitions played in Furball's small head as she surveyed the yard and the other creatures in it. She must have scuttled back inside the shed, since after a while she opened her eyes and found herself curled up into a ball and lying underneath one of the deckchairs, right at the back of the shed. She had forgotten going to the back of the shed, forgotten curling up, forgotten falling asleep – but then, a hamster cannot be expected to think of everything. Falling asleep had somehow involved getting covered in dust, so that, being a clean-minded little hamster, she had to go through the washing routine all over again. Lick paws. Shut eyes. Wipe face. Wipe ears. Busy life, a hamster's.

When she was clean once more, she padded towards the hole, and daylight. First nose, then whiskers were pushed outside. She looked towards the tree. There was no sign of the snark. No claws to be seen. Distantly, she could hear a snarl yapping, but distantly. There were other noises – ooms with their machines whirring and roaring and moving in their mysterious way. Two ooms in bright yellow shiny hats were calling to one another, as fevvas do. They had a small box from which more calling was coming – it was like the noise-box which the Giant's mum and dad had in their kitchen. Overhead in the great Blue, more ooms roared about in their great metal fevvas. But the yard itself looked safe.

Furball had woken up with a terrible hunger. She had somehow expected the Giant to bring food to her in the shed. Now she knew there was something wrong with this idea. The Giant had *not* brought food. The Giant had probably put food in the cage but… No, it was all too complicated for Furball. And she simply never thought that the Giant might not know where she was.

The chief thing now was hunger. Food. Seeds. Must have food. She sniffed the air, and then, forgetting the dangers of the yard, she simply ran towards Lundine, hoping she'd pass the patch of ground where the snark had spilled so many seeds. Failing that, she'd run back to Lundine, though she had, for the moment, forgotten where to find the hole that led there. But first things first. *Seeds, seeds, seeds.*

She scampered all over the yard, moving as fast as she could. And she didn't hear the heavy thud of oom shoes until a shadow fell over her. There was no way she could have escaped. A big oom hand came down on and squeezed her ribs tightly. Lifted high into the air, she heard an oom voice cry out, 'What have we here!'

CHAPTER TEN

This is War

'You can see how pleased I am, Mister Peter. This sandwich is truly delicious.'

The Giant was saying this in her high-pitched Chum voice, which made everyone laugh.

The hand which, some time ago now, had found Chum in the garden, had been Mum's hand. Chum had been returned to her cage and to celebrate, Kitty had bought a huge hamster treat from the shop. A mass of seeds wedged together in honey formed something in the shape of a sandwich.

'Thank you *so* much, Giant,' squeaked Kitty to herself, and to Mum and Dad, in her Chum voice.

'How on earth did you get out into the garden,

Chum?' The question was Dad's.

'I hope you weren't worried, Mister Peter,' was the high-pitched reply.

And they all laughed.

When Kitty had stopped speaking in her Chum voice, when she had gone upstairs to play on dad's computer, Mum called after her, 'No playing on the computer.'

'It's called homework, Mum. Like – I need to finish my project.'

'I thought your project was *observation* – looking at the real world!' Mum called back.

Kitty's school project was a survey of the variety of birds to be seen in the course of one month in a small London garden. She had made a few notes based on what she saw from the window, and from Mum's bird books. Mum couldn't see why Kitty needed a computer for this project. Surely the whole point of it was to use her eyes and ears, to look at real birds in a real garden, to recognise finches and tits and robins for herself, not just look them up on a screen. But Kitty couldn't imagine doing anything without a computer.

'There's always my encyclopedia,' Dad called up the stairs, as Kitty opened his laptop and began to call up her friends on Facebook.

When Kitty's parents were alone together, Mum said, 'They're back in force. You must have noticed.'

Dad grunted from behind his newspaper.

'You saw all the droppings in the larder, and it's started to stink in there. Last time we had to take out every single packet of food. They'd eaten their way through the pasta, and the biscuits. They'd even nibbled into the packet of porridge.'

The newspaper rustled. A sound like *hrrumff* came from behind it.

'They won't just go away, Peter.'

'Oh, *Alexandra*.' Dad always used Mum's full name when he was annoyed.

'It isn't fair if I have to do everything. You and Kitty don't clear up the mess. You and Kitty won't move every single packet of dried food off those shelves, and wipe them clean, and disinfect the floor. It's a mouse toilet that place.'

'What do you suggest we do?' asked Dad, at long

last putting down his newspaper.

'We have got to find where they live, how they get into the kitchen and larder. We must block up the holes.'

'Starve them out?'

'They're a health hazard, Peter. They're vermin. One of them came in and stood on my foot yesterday, while I was having coffee at this very table. It *stared* at me.'

Kitty's dad held his paper up but couldn't hide his snort of laughter.

'*Peter!*' shrieked Kitty's mum. 'This is *war*!'

The newspaper quivered. 'War?'

'Yes!' Kitty's mum stood up. 'We're under siege, Peter. The mice have to go! We need to set traps.'

'That seems a bit drastic.'

'Alan and Rupert put down sticky-traps. They say it's the only way.'

'How do they work exactly?'

'The mice step on them and get stuck. They can't move.'

'And then you kill them?'

'That's *your* job,' she said.

'I don't think…' Dad began.

But Mum stood firm. 'It's us or them, Peter! It's not just one or two of them – it's an invasion.'

Kitty's dad sighed.

CHAPTER ELEVEN

Ooms Alert!

The mokes still visited Furball. But for some time now, she had noticed that Mokey Moke was getting fat. Unlike Furball, with the mass of fur that gave her her new name, the mokes were lean and their bones showed through their short grey-black fur. Their pointy faces were thin. But now Mokey Moke was swollen up and looked very fat indeed.

Buster and Nobby tried to explain things. But this left Furball even more confused.

'Mum's up the duff,' Nobby said.

'Got six to feed, she says,' laughed Buster.

'Who's Mum?' asked Furball.

She'd never thought about the mokes having

relatives before. She herself had once had a mother, and brothers and sisters. Long ago in a pet shop. They had all nestled together in some straw until they were scooped out and sold to different human families. So Furball had grown up alone, with no idea what a big family might be like.

'Are you in the same family?' she asked now.

'All are,' said Buster. 'Nobby's me bruvver, inny –'

'Sure fing, Furball,' said Nobby. 'And now ole Mum's up the duff agin and there'll be more of us like.'

'Where is the duff?' asked Furball.

The two young mice laughed. But they laughed at everything, even food. And now they looked expectantly at Furball's seed sandwich.

'We couldn't elp noticing.'

'Couldn't elp it could we, Furb?'

'You mean this huge sandwich?'

Furball had pouched, and then eaten, about a quarter of the seed sandwich the Giant had bought her. 'Do you want to share it?' she said kindly.

Nobby had come to the lower door of the cage. Its

clasp had loosened since the days when Murphy lived in it. Furball could now open it with ease, and even Nobby and Buster with their mouse paws could push it open once Furball had done the difficult part.

'Only,' said Nobby, 'like we say, six to feed, now Mokey Moke's spectin.'

'Specting? Inspecting? What is inspecting?'

'Ex. *Ex*,' said Nobby patiently. '*Ex*pectin – only –'

'Might not be six. Might be four,' said Buster.

'Don't know till they come, see.'

'Yes,' said Furball. 'I see.' But she didn't.

'If you was to help us eave some of that seed sandwich behind the dresser, like.'

'Is that where the duff is?'

'She's a card,' laughed Buster.

About half the sandwich was still stuck together. Furball opened her cage door, and hurled it out, so it fell with a clatter on to the kitchen floor.

'Eave – eave!' called Nobby and Buster. And Furball called back 'Heave!'

The door of the cage, with its loose fastening, shut behind Furball.

When they had all three scuttered down from the ledge where Furball's cage was balanced, Furball was the first to rejoin the sandwich in the middle of the kitchen floor.

'That'll keep Mum going,' Nobby grinned.

'Six ter feed,' Buster squeaked.

'Only she didn't feel like coming out today – not with being near her time.'

Furball absent-mindedly bit a corner of the sandwich and pouched it. It was difficult to speak with her pouch full but she managed to ask, 'Near what time?'

Nobby and Buster squeaked with giggles.

'She don't get it.'

'Some as lives too long with ooms lose touch with ow the rest of us live, like.'

'Stir rots yer brain.'

This could have been, but the mokes really liked her and were just teasing her, the way they talked to each other.

'She can't get out much now she's near her time,' said Nobby.

'Mokey Moke's knocked up,' added his brother.

'Got a bun in the oven,' said Nobby, in a tone which suggested you could not get clearer than this.

If Mokey Moke already had a bun, Furball wondered why she would need this sandwich. But she didn't ask any more questions because she didn't want to seem foolish. She didn't understand what Nobby and Buster were talking about, and she knew that they *knew*. She wished they wouldn't tease her about it so much, though. Mokey Moke was her closest friend among the mokes. It was clear that something important was happening to her. And Furball didn't like the sound of being knocked up, or up the duff, whatever this was. But if she had a bun, then this extra sandwich would be useful if she somehow had as many as six to feed.

'Now for a good ole eave-o,' said Buster.

'Ere goes.'

'It would be quicker…' But Furball still had her mouth full of sandwich and couldn't speak clearly. She wanted to say that she could drag the sandwich without help from the young mokes.

'Wozzat Furb, ole pal?'

'I said…' But it sounded like – *Mum* – *wah splursh mm wah.*

'Good on yer.'

'Thassa girl.'

Nobby had clumsily grabbed one side of the sandwich in his paws, while Buster tried to hold the other side with his teeth. It looked as if they would end up having a tug of war with the thing, that it would come to bits and they'd end up making several journeys with crumbs and sandwich bits to the mouse hole under the dresser. Rather than explaining this to them, she picked up the whole sandwich in her teeth and pulled, and just as she feared – it broke into several pieces on the kitchen floor.

'Now look wotcha gunnun dun.'

'Blimey!' Nobby was giggling as usual.

Ignoring them, Furball picked up the largest piece and ran under the dresser with it, placing it on the floor by the skirting board near the hole they came through to the kitchen. She clambered up the skirting board with the sandwich piece in her mouth, but it was too big to fit through the hole and she slithered down to the floor again, landing with a thud on her bottom. She pondered. She could either break the sandwich into smaller pieces and post them through the slit at the top of the skirting board. Or she could leave it on the floor under the dresser, hoping Mokey Moke would come down from the duff to eat. Or Furball could pouch the lot and make another attempt to squeeze through the hole. She didn't think of leaving the sandwich piece where it was. The humans hardly ever cleaned under the dresser, so it would have stayed there until the mokes had eaten it. But Furball followed her instincts and, without further thought, pouched the large sticky slice of seeds.

This gave her the biggest 'hammer head' she'd ever had. She tried to clamber up the skirting board again to squeeze through the hole but when she reached the top she could sense, even in the darkness, there was no possibility she could squeeze through so narrow a slit.

Meanwhile, in the middle of the floor, Buster and Nobby had forgotten they were meant to be working. They had nibbled a few honey-coated seeds from the broken sandwich. That was nice. Then Nobby thought it would be fun to flick Buster with sticky crumbs.

And after he had been pelted with two or three of these missiles, Buster thought it would be much funnier to flick crumbs at Nobby. And Nobby flicked back at Buster and Buster at Nobby, while crumbs and seeds flew everywhere.

They squeaked so happily that Furball was tempted to join in. But something, some inner instinct, warned her they shouldn't neglect the task in hand, that they ought to drag as much of the sandwich as possible to the safety and darkness under the dresser. By now she was too heavily pouched to speak, so she just watched the young mokes laughing and flicking and shouting.

'You're *covered* in it –'

'Look at you, mate!'

It was true. Both young mokes had seed and honey stuck to their thin backs and boney flanks.

They were enjoying themselves so much that they barely heard the heavy human footsteps in the hall, until Buster dropped his piece and squealed out.

'Ooms alert – ooms alert!'

As the olive-green Converse several times larger

than a hamster, and much larger than a mouse, came into view on the kitchen floor, the mokes knew they had been seen. Kitty's mum was yelling.

'*MICE!*'

CHAPTER TWELVE

Mice Rights

Kitty's mum didn't know the clasp on the hamster cage was loose. Or that Chum could leave it whenever she chose. Even the young mice could open it. Of course, when Chum left her cage, the door-flap closed and the clasp closed with it. So, the cage looked just as if Chum was safe inside it with the doors locked. If Kitty's mum had been looking at the cage, which she was not, she would have seen nothing to make her suspect it was unoccupied. There were many hours of the day when Chum hid away in the dark and warmth and safety of the bedroom (a sort of plastic box with a lid on it), where she slept in comfort in Dad's sock – a soft, green cashmere sock full of holes, covered with flecks of sawdust, with a comforting hamster smell.

But at that moment, Kitty's mum had forgotten about Chum. She just knew she hated sharing her home with mice. Kitty's mum wasn't scared of mice, but she hated what they did. She hated them chewing through food packets on the larder shelves. She hated the mess this made. She hated them using her kitchen and her larder and the hall outside the kitchen as their lavatory. She hated the little mouse droppings and crumbs and bits of half-chewed cardboard which they left behind them. And she hated the smell.

At present there was a very bad smell – a pong, in fact, as Kitty said. And it pointed to two mouse areas: one just near a corner of the kitchen dresser and one near the bottom of the stairs.

'They've obviously made an underground passage,' said Kitty's mum to Dad and Kitty at supper one day. 'They come out of the hole at the bottom of the stairs and run into the larder. Then they run across the kitchen. I saw one of the little beggars *on top of the fridge* yesterday.'

Dad took a great interest in his food at this point.

He didn't seem to hear what Mum was saying.

'You have to admit it was clever,' said Kitty. 'Those *tiny* little mice, climbing up to the top of the fridge.'

'I don't have to admit any such thing,' said her mother.

Mum was annoyed that neither Kitty nor Dad would help with the mouse problem. Dad refused to talk about it. In Mum's opinion, he would pretend a menace wasn't there – until it was too late. But Kitty was even worse, thought Mum. In fact, Kitty had even said, 'The mice have as much right to be here as we have.'

'Oh, *great*,' her mum had said. 'So now we have Mice Rights.'

Dad broke his silence on the matter and said, 'Kitty could be right. I mean, what makes it all right for us to be here but not the mice? Who said that human beings are lords of the universe? What about a bit of live and let live?'

'Yeah, *Mum*,' Kitty had added, with such strong emphasis on the word *Mum* that it sounded like an accusation.

'I don't barge in on the mice and steal their food,' said Mum. 'Or make a mess and a stink where they live.' She stamped her foot. 'Oh, this is *stupid*! Neither of you cleans up after them. I'm the one who always does it. And it's *got to stop*.'

Every time they talked about mice, this is how it ended.

So Kitty's mum talked with the neighbours. Anne-next-door-but-one recommended an electrical device that made vibrations the mice didn't like, so they just moved on.

'No little corpses under the sink, no smelly dead bodies,' said Anne. 'They just *go*. One minute, a plague, the next – peace!'

But the neighbours called Alan and Rupert said when *they* tried these devices, they didn't work at all.

Some people suggested ringing up the council. But Kitty's mum had tried ringing the council once before.

They had sent a man who put down pots of poisonous sludge at various points. It was not completely unsuccessful. Although most of the poisoned food was left untasted, there were signs, in one plastic plate of poison, of paw marks. Some of the food had been eaten.

Nothing happened for about two weeks; but gradually the most appalling smell began to waft from behind the dishwasher. When the smell changed from bad to unbearable, the white metal dishwasher was moved away from the wall and there they had found an enormous dead rat, which had clearly eaten the poison. In life, rats pong. In death, they do more: the stink is so strong you want to throw up.

All this meant that Kitty's mum no longer believed in the electrical device and she definitely didn't want the smell of poisoned bodies. The only options left were traps. There were old-fashioned mousetraps – pieces of wood with springs fastened to them. A bit of cheese tempted the mice on to the wood. But when a mouse came to eat the cheese, it set off the spring and a metal bar snapped sharply down on its body, killing it instantly.

Mum found that idea upsetting. She didn't want Kitty to see squashed mouse bodies in the kitchen, at the bottom of the stairs, or in the larder.

This just left the so-called 'sticky-traps'. Rupert, who recommended them, said that his friend Alan believed them to be the best way – 'the only way'. Mum didn't want to know how the sticky-traps worked. She simply told Kitty's dad that if she put these traps down, he would have to 'deal with' any mice they caught. He had sighed, but reluctantly agreed.

Their last discussion about sticky-traps had been the previous evening after Kitty went to bed.

'You'd have to make sure Chum was in her cage,' said Kitty's dad.

'Of course I would.'

'Only, it would be awful, if we put one of these – these *things* on the floor and Chum got stuck on it.'

'Peter, I'm not an idiot.'

And now, Kitty's mum had been to the hardware shop and bought several sticky-traps for the mice. She had walked into the kitchen and seen the mess – seeds and stickiness and mouse droppings under the table.

Now she was going to use the sticky-traps.

She swept all of the mess into a dustpan and emptied it into the rubbish bin. She didn't recognise the remains of the sandwich Kitty had bought to celebrate Chum's return. But she did remember to be careful, before laying the traps, that Chum was safe in her cage. She looked at the cage on its shelf. The two cage doors were shut. There was no sign of Chum, which usually meant she was curled up, warmly asleep in Peter's sock at the bottom of the cage.

Mum took a packet out of her shopping bag and read the instructions. It seemed very straightforward. She removed the outer wrapping and exposed the sticky floor of the tray. Then she placed the plastic tray, which was about the size of a small paperback book, in a spot where she thought the mice went.

The first trap was easy – the larder shelf next to the cereal packets, where she found holes nibbled in packets of Coco-Pops and porridge boxes. She placed the tray with the quiet concentration of a general planning an attack on the battlefield.

Then she thought she'd put one tray at each of the two entrances from the mouse world to her own, that is, at the bottom of the stairs and under the dresser. It felt a bit gruesome, but once she had caught a few mice, the others would surely get the message and move somewhere, *anywhere* – just as long as it was away from here.

CHAPTER THIRTEEN

The New Rivals

'Maybe if we broke it up.'

'Couldn't you pouch it, Furball?'

'I did pouch some of it.'

Furball felt too shy to admit that the bit of seed sandwich in her pouch had tasted so delicious that she had quietly de-pouched and eaten most of it.

She and the two mokes were hiding under the dresser. They had managed to drag most of the sandwich across the floor. From where they crouched, they could see the Converse of the Giant's mum moving about the room. They heard angry noises as she swept up the crumbs from under the table.

Buster said, 'Reckon vats floor-flood what she's

puttin' vere.'

Nobby and Furball had been concentrating on how to get the various pieces of honey-coated seed through the gap at the top of the skirting board. They had paid much attention to the Giant's mum.

'Remember olc Uncle Barney?' Buster said.

'*Buster*,' said Nobby. 'We're trying to take food to Mum.'

'Up the duff,' suggested Furball, without knowing what she meant. The two mokes ignored this.

'And all you can do is talk bout Uncle Barney and the flippin floor-food.'

'Wanna watch wot you eat off floor,' said Buster.

'Yeah. Well.' Nobby agreed.

'See vat tray vere…'

Buster was so persistent that for a moment the others abandoned the sandwich problem and came to the edge of the dresser, to the part of the floor in daylight. Not far away, in the corner of the dresser nearest the kitchen window, was a small yellow tray – large enough, say, for four hamsters to stand together on it, side by side. It had a springy-looking yellow surface, a bit like a carpet. Furball thought it looked a *comfortable* sort of thing, something a hamster could *play* on.

'Vat tray,' said Buster. 'See it.'

Nobby admitted he could see it.

'She put vat tray darn,' said Buster. 'Now, the other one, the one wot Furball calls Giant –'

'The Giant,' agreed Furball. 'She's *very nice*. I'm sure she would feed us *all* if she could. That's why I've had this idea that we could all live together, in the shed outside Lundine...'

But Buster wasn't listening. If he had listened, he wouldn't have believed it for a moment. As if any oom, even the Giant, would offer food and shelter to all the Lundine mokes – that wasn't what ooms did.

'The Giant,' Buster continued. 'Now the Giant, I grantcha. She might – I'm only saying might mind – might put darn food which weren't floor-food. No stuff. No stuff wot Uncle Barney et, know whaddeye mean. Safe food. But Ole Converse. Old Gym-shoes...'

'Giant's mum,' said Furball. She felt suddenly that she missed the Giant. Standing there in the half-shadows under the dresser, and hearing Buster talk in tense, excited tones about the dangers of being at large, she thought how much she'd like to be held in the Giant's gentle hands, to run up her jumper, down her sleeve, and to poke out her pink nose and wiggle her whiskers while all the ooms exclaimed, 'Chum! Chum!'

'Ole Gym-shoes put food darn for mokes?' Buster was saying. 'Don't make me larf. Nar. Vat tray. I'm not saying it's floor-food exactly. Not as such. But vere's sommat not right. Know whaddeye mean?'

Furball didn't know what Buster meant. The tray-carpet (or trampoline perhaps?) looked like a toy which the Giant's mum had kindly placed on the floor. It seemed quite harmless to Furball.

Nobby, who stood beside her, had become tense. He clenched and unclenched his paws.

'Mebbe Buster's right nall.'

'I do not think,' said Furball coldly, 'that the Giant's mum would do anything to harm me.'

'Mebbe not *you*, Furba – but *mokes*. Mokes is different. She'd do summat to arm mokes. Never forget Uncle Barney. Now e et floor-flood. Not sayin it were put darn by Giant-mum. But by an *oom*. And e copped it.'

'Not forgettin Aunty Flo in the snapper,' said Buster.

'Splat she went,' said Nobby.

'I'm sure you're wrong,' said Furball. 'Anyway, I never met your Uncle Barney and your Aunty Flo. They're only stories.'

'Yeah,' said Nobby. 'Only stories – like Ole Murph what the ooms put in ole, filled it with mud. Only stories. Only see it wiv me own eyes.'

There was silence as the three of them stared at the little tray. Furball knew she was right. She knew the Giant's mum would never, *ever* do anything to harm her. She was on the point of proving the mokes wrong, showing them the new tray was harmless, possibly even a toy, by running out and playing on it, when Buster said, 'Anyway, Furball ole girl, ow bart the grub ven?'

'Grub.'

'Give sandwich ole eave-oh.'

After several unsuccessful attempts to squeeze the largest piece of sandwich through the slit at the top of the skirting board, they decided to break it up into small pieces. This was easy for Furball since she was much larger and a better climber than the mokes. Then she pouched what she could, climbed the skirting board once more, and with much squeezing and pushing and puffing and panting, managed to drop herself down in the grey dark dust on the other side.

'Mum's garn deepest Lundine,' Nobby said, leading the way.

(Kitty's mum had been right – there was a passage under the kitchen floor which led from the dresser to the bottom of the stairs.)

Furball was good at burrowing and she was used to darkness, but she didn't like the tunnel. It was dirty and dusty and smelly. It was horrid. So she was surprised when Nobby put down his bit of sandwich and exclaimed, 'Good old Lundine!'

Buster, too, paused for breath and agreed. 'You feel safe in here.'

Furball wondered if they were taking her up the duff, where they'd said Mokey Moke had gone – because she was 'spectin'. But every time she talked about it with them, the mokes had squeaked with such wild laughter that she was too shy to say any more. She didn't know what they meant or what was going on in Mokey Moke's life, and this made her feel foolish. So she said nothing while the two mokes enjoyed the warm, choking, dusty air. And when they skipped onwards, she followed.

They scuttled and jumped and ran in short darts for what seemed a long time, until Nobby put down his sandwich and squeaked – '*Mum!*'

'*Ere,*' came the familiar voice of Mokey Moke through the shadows.

'Broughta vister,' squeaked Nobby, with Buster adding, 'Nice sprise ferya.'

'Vister,' squeaked Nobby again.

'Oozat ven?' called Mokey Moke.

All the mokes laughed. Once again, Furball was glad she hadn't said anything to make her seem foolish.

'Can't guess!' Mokey Moke was saying.

'Real mystery! Now *oo* could it be?' laughed Buster.

In the darkness there were squeakings from a number of mokes. The commotion set off a chorus of very high-pitched moke voices. The noise was almost like the song of the fevvas in the backyard which Furball had heard on her shed adventure.

Mokey Moke was lying in an improvised nest. Furball, Nobby and Buster had scuttled the whole length of the underground passage beneath the kitchen floor. They had reached an area beneath the bottom of the stairs, leading out to the kitchen corridor, and through a gap in the bottom stair soft grey light glimmered on to the scene.

And where Mokey Moke lay in her nest, there were two tiny pinkish-grey mokes nestling at her stomach, sucking her milk. Beside them two other mokes, equally tiny, equally pink, were squeaking that it was their turn to feed.

'Well ere's a turn-up for the books, Mum,' said Nobby.

'Who's vey ven?' laughed Buster. 'Arencha gointer intradjuice-us?'

'These are the new Arrivals,' said Mokey Moke proudly.

'Only,' said Nobby, 'Some of us call em The Rivals.'

It was extraordinary. Furball looked at the thin, but beautiful, little moke babies and wondered where they had come from. Were these what Mokey Moke had been 'spectin'?

'Have you been to the pet shop?' she asked politely.

All the mokes squawked with laughter.

'Vat's right,' said Mokey Moke. 'Reckon I got a good bargain, eh – gottem free.'

'We brought you this seed sandwich,' said Furball.

Almost before she had placed the sticky slab in the dust, mokes from all sides gathered round to grab and bite into it. She approached Mokey Moke and de-pouched some more, then held it out in her clean pink paws for her friend as she lay there, feeding her babies.

'You're a good pal, Furball,' said Mokey Moke.

'Said old Furball would see us right, Mum,' said Nobby.

Then Mokey Moke explained that the mokes had become hungry when she couldn't go with them on food raids. They had a rule – every moke for hisself. It meant that no moke depended on another for food. But in practice the young mokes relied on Mokey Moke to lead them, to show them the best places for supplies. And Mokey Moke kept them in good order. She'd organise two mokes as lookouts, and the others into climbing parties to fetch food from shelves. But when the food supply dried up, several of the mokes had gone missing, she'd said.

'You must be worried,' said Furball.

'Not exactly,' said Mokey Moke. 'You can't keep an eye on em all. Just you wonder where some on them get to.' Then she looked down at her babies and said, 'That's enough for you two Arrivals. Ere. Gerroff. Let someone else ave-a suck for a change.'

'Would they like some of this?' asked Furball, holding out in her paw some of the sandwich she had de-pouched.

'That's kind of you, love – but leave it a while, eh. They're a bit young for solids.'

CHAPTER FOURTEEN

A Really Worrying Time

'Where's Chum?' asked Kitty.

'Wherever you last left her,' said her mum.

'*Mu-er-umum!*'

'She won't have gone far,' said Mum.

The whole evening was spent searching for the hamster. It was almost becoming a routine.

'She's always come back in the past,' said Dad as he kissed Kitty goodnight.

Later, when they were in bed together, Mum said to Dad, 'I didn't tell Kitty about the traps.'

'And you're sure you've picked them all up – you haven't left a trap down there by mistake?'

'There was one by the bottom of the stairs and one

in the larder,' mum said.

It had been a tiring evening, with the hamster on the run yet again. Mum had remembered to pick up two of the traps she had laid. With all the worry – blaming herself for not checking whether Chum was in her cage, trying to calm Kitty, quarrelling with Dad – she forgot about the third sticky-trap, the one under the dresser.

A really worrying time can keep you awake all night. Or it can exhaust you. Kitty's mum fell into a deep sleep!

CHAPTER FIFTEEN

Twelve Paws are Better Than Four

'They'll soon be big enough to get food their selves,' said Mokey Moke. 'Dusna take long wean a moke.'

As mother of the new Arrivals, she ignored all Furball's questions about how the little mokes had arrived. Furball was puzzled by the whole business, but found that Mokey Moke wouldn't let her into the secret. When she asked Nobby and Buster if the pet shop man had brought the young mokes, Nobby had agreed, and said, 'Oh that's right, Buster – eh?'

And Buster said, 'Bring em round in a van, dinny? Drove up into Lundine easy. Passed iz van. Carried out The Rivals. Lovely.'

Furball joined in the laughter. She was a very polite hamster.

But she didn't understand the joke, and her failure to understand made her feel foolish. The mokes could be rather patronising. Furball only half liked it when they said, 'Good ole Furbs,' or 'She's better than a show she is.'

But when Furball offered to search for more food, everything was different. The mokes all agreed that no one could pouch a good bit of grub like old Furba. And because she was glad they were pleased, Furball set off once more down the long dusty corridor.

Nobby and Buster offered to join her, and since twelve paws are better than four, she had happily agreed. Besides, Nobby and Buster were now her best friends, and she loved their company, even if their jokes about The Rivals puzzled her.

Furball scudded purposefully down the corridor, intent on reaching the hole under the dresser in as short a time as possible. Nobby and Buster, as always, did things differently. Sometimes Nobby ran ahead. Sometimes he held a bundle of fluff above his head and pretended it was a grey wig.

'Oi'm ole Granny Moke. Hello, Furball my dear,' he quavered. Sometimes, waving the same bit of grey fluff, he danced up behind her, squeaking and pretending to be the grey moke-ghostie of ole Lundinc Town.

Buster played games too. Because they frolicked and danced backwards and forwards and sideways and back, they must have run three times as far as Furball, and when she reached the hole in the skirting board under the dresser she had to wait for them to catch up. She squeezed through the gap and let herself down in the darkness to the kitchen floor.

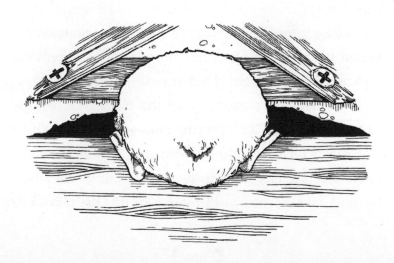

CHAPTER SIXTEEN

Stuck on a Rock

In her very deep sleep, Kitty's mum was still worrying about the mousetraps. There was a bit of her brain that was still awake. But she was still asleep, and in the middle of a dream about people who play no part in this story.

These people were swimming in the sea, near the beach where Kitty with her mum and dad went on holiday. In the dream, Dad was standing on a rock, yelling. His foot was stuck to the rock, as if it was glued there. He was crying and screaming. Mum woke up. Her first thought was: *typical of Peter to put his foot in the one trap on the beach.* Then she asked herself: *Did I pick up all the sticky-traps downstairs?*

What about the one under the dresser? She decided to look for that one in the morning.

CHAPTER SEVENTEEN

Rich Tea Biscuits
& Pearl Barley

Furball and the young mokes entered the kitchen. They all knew their way around and Furball set out purposefully across the kitchen to edge her way through the larder door. If the larder door wasn't open (and it usually was), then they would find food in another place. On the dresser itself was the ledge where the Giant kept the packet of hamster food. It was a big climb, but if she needed to shimmy up the dresser she would (just) be able to do it.

While she was having these practical and purposeful thoughts, her two young friends were racing round and round in circles under the dresser. None of them, as yet, had seen the sticky-trap on the floor, halfway out from under the dresser. After running round in circles, Nobby and Buster were out of breath. Nobby paused and let a few little dark brown, almost black droppings fall on the kitchen floor before scampering off once more.

'Perhaps – the larder…' said Furball, in her quiet little voice.

'Wozzat?' called Buster.

'Perhaps the larder.'

'Oh –' in their bad imitation of her voice – 'Per heps the lah-de-da.'

Furball scuttled straight towards the larder door with the speed of an electric toy. By the time Buster and Nobby pranced up behind, Furball was calling, 'We're in luck – the door is open.'

The thought of the six new Rivals, and of Mokey Moke needing more food, inspired Furball to real hard work. She climbed into the plastic shopping basket on the larder floor, although once at the bottom of the basket, she found it impossible to resist a nibble at a particularly succulent carrot.

'We have here – carrots – potatoes.'

'Any biskoes in there, Furbs?'

'Not that I can see,' she called back. She was already clambering out, heaving a carrot in her mouth, when Nobby repeated his biscuit request. Furball didn't admit she wasn't sure what a 'bisko' was.

Furball was much bigger than the mokes, and she was a much better climber. But sometimes, when they broke into laughter, she still wondered if they were making fun of her. But she knew they really did admire her skills as a climber, and as a food carrier. So it pleased her to show off, just a little, to Nobby and Buster.

The two young mokes stood on the larder floor and watched her climb up the wall to the shelf. For them it was as exciting as an evening at the circus. Furball's small pink paws, with their sharp-clawed fingers, carried her up the sheer brick face of the larder wall. Then with a heave – heave – HEAVE, she was on the shelf.

Nobby and Buster stared up at her. In their sharp grey faces and jet-black shining eyes she could see sheer admiration.

'Good on yer, Furb.'

'Cor – see the way she took that wall?'

'Like yer footwork, Furb.'

Of course, they laughed as they said this – they always laughed, whatever they said, just as they never made a journey without leaping about making everything into a game. Still they were clearly impressed – very impressed indeed, and for Furball this felt very good.

She called down to them. 'Plenty up here!'

She reached out with her paws, and a long shining blue tower labelled RICH TEA BISCUITS tottered over and almost squashed her on the spot. As it rolled off the shelf, faster and faster, it could have squashed all of them, but Nobby and Buster liked to live dangerously and they danced out of the way as the blue packet fell to the floor. Once it had landed, they ran towards it and began to nibble the shiny packaging.

'Nuff ter keep us goin forever ere, Furball.'

'We'll drag it back under the dresser,' she called down from the shelf. 'While I'm up here – anything else you'd like?'

Now she was showing off with a stylish hamster dance as she reached for different packets. From a packet of rice, a pattering rain dropped on the shelf and floor. From another packet, labelled PEARL BARLEY, she gobbled a pouchful of hard but tasty little nuggets.

'Is it my burfdie or summat?' asked Nobby as some of the pearl barley bounced towards his head.

Furball was saying, 'Or there are raisins…' These were delicious. She ate several and threw a few more over the edge.

'I reckon you've got us what I never fort we'd ave,' called Buster.

'Bisker?' asked Furball nonchalantly, hoping she'd got the word right.

'Better than that, Furb – nuff!'

Nobby squeaked with delight at this. 'Never thought we'd ave nuff.'

With no idea what they were talking about, Furball joined in the laughter.

Now it was time to begin her descent. Peeping over the edge of the shelf she felt as if she was looking over a really high cliff. Nobby and Buster weren't watching now. They were attacking the Rich Tea biscuits packet with a frenzy, spitting out wrapping and munching the biscuits. Very gingerly, Furball put her paws on the edge of the shelf and swung herself over.

CHAPTER EIGHTEEN

Can't We Wait Until Morning?

Two floors up, Kitty's parents lay side by side in bed. Dad was snoring. Perhaps it was this which woke Mum, but it felt like the twentieth time she'd woken that night.

'Peter.'

Dad made various noises which sounded like a pig trying to get comfortable in its straw.

'Peter.'

He mumbled, then said, 'Bad dream?'

'Peter.'

Suddenly he sat up, in a panic. 'Burglars? Fire? Flood?'

'It's those sticky-traps.'

He groaned.

'I don't think I picked up the sticky-trap under the dresser,' she said.

'You probably did.'

'But I'm not *sure.*'

'Go down and check if you're so worried.'

'I don't want to.'

'Why not?'

''Cause if Chum… if Chum *has* got caught in it… You don't think she has, do you?'

'How can I know whether the hamster has got caught in a mousetrap?'

'Go and look. *Please.*'

'What if she has? What if the hamster is caught in this – this *sticky*-trap. Can we get her out of it?'

Mum was silent.

'I could take her to the vet in the morning, I suppose.' He groaned again. 'But I've got so much work tomorrow and – what *time* is it?'

'Twenty to three.'

'Can't we wait until morning?' he asked. 'Or should I say – until a bit *later* this morning.'

'We can't let Kitty see,' said his wife. 'If Chum's stuck in the trap, we'll have to… you'll have to…'

'I've *said* – I'll take her to the vet.'

'Peter, a vet won't be any good. You haven't looked at those traps. They are designed to catch extremely lively rodents. They'll put their feet on them and never get them off. Never. If Chum's walked on the trap, she'll just be stuck on it. She'll never escape from it. You understand what I'm saying.'

'*Please*… can't we talk about it in the morning?'

'In front of Kitty? No. You have to go down there.'

'What – now?'

'Maybe not now, but before Kitty wakes up. If Chum's stuck in the trap, you'll have to… oh, this is *awful*.'

'You're saying I'll have to kill Chum?'

'You'll have to get rid of her before Kitty wakes up. We'll say she's just lost, gone missing. We'll promise her a new hamster… a dog…'

'Why don't *you* kill the hamster? You're the one who put down the trap!'

'Oh, Pete, don't be mean – it's awful. We're all in this together.'

'OK. In the morning, I'll do something. OK? I'll go down and make us all a nice cup of tea. And if I find Chum has been caught in the trap I'll…'

'Thanks.' She squeezed his hand in the darkness.

About half an hour later when Mum was asleep, he asked aloud, 'What? If I find Chum has been caught in the trap, I'll what? I can't squash her or drown her or flush her down the toilet… She's family.'

And he groaned.

CHAPTER NINETEEN

The Fear

Thanks to Furball, it was a truly magnificent haul.

'Wiv vis little lot we'll be larfin all the way till Lord Mayor's Showdie,' said Buster.

Nobby was still enjoying his brother's earlier joke. 'We've got nuff. Never ad nuff before. Furball's as got us what we never ad fore. Nuff.'

'It's a good one, eh,' agreed Buster.

Furball concentrated on heaving the packet of biscuits across the kitchen floor. It was bigger than she was but because it was a cylinder she could roll it, at least for some of the way. Buster and Nobby said they would help, but they kept getting distracted. At one point they ran back into the larder to nibble at the grains of pearl barley on the floor. Then they'd remember that old Furball was struggling and they would dance back to put their shoulders against the biscuit packet.

'Only,' puffed Nobby, 'shame ter leave all vat stuff byind.'

'If we get this rolled under the dresser,' puffcd Furball, 'we can come back for more.'

'Ow gonna get froo ole?' asked Nobby. Furball had to admit, she hadn't asked herself the question. How *would* they squeeze the large biscuit packet through the quite small crack at the top of the skirting board under the dresser? Just get the packet rolled out of oom sight – that was her scheme.

It was a hard struggle, and a long one, but eventually they did it. They were safc under the dresser. The packet of biscuits was theirs. If they told Mokey Moke of their triumph, she would probably organize as many as ten mokes to help carry the biscuits to the nest.

Furball ran about excitedly under the dresser. She ran this way and that, sometimes thinking about the biscuits and sometimes thinking of nothing, just enjoying the freedom to scuttle about.

She came to a plastic tray, halfway under the dresser and halfway out. It had a rather pleasant smell, and for a moment she thought of how nice it was to snuggle under the Giant's jumper. Was this tray some food which had been kindly placed there by the Giant? Or was it a game, such as the wheel which the Giant sometimes placed in her cage? She edged forward and sniffed the tray. It smelt a little bit like nuts. Not at all unpleasing.

'Wotcha found there ven, Furbs?' asked Nobby. He came bounding up behind her, and jumped recklessly on to the tray.

'I don't know,' said Furball.

'It's a stuck-up,' said Nobby. 'Get back – get back. Buster, don't come on vis whaddever yer do, mate! Furbs, stand back – I got blooming stuck, en I?'

Furball was so used to Nobby making jokes that for a while she found didn't realise that this was something serious, deadly serious. She moved towards the tray to help him and he began to squeal in an agonised high-pitched tone which she'd never heard before.

'Stand back! Stand back! It's a trap, innit – an oom trap!'

'I'll go fer elp, mate,' said Buster.

'Don't let no more mokes on ere – it's a trap,' gasped Nobby.

'I'll get Mokey Moke – she'll know what to do.'

'Don't let no Rivals on ere, mate – they'll be stuck an all.'

Buster disappeared down the hole at the top of the skirting board. Furball simply stared, her whiskers quivering with horror, at Nobby's face as he stared back at her. Nobby had often puzzled her, or said things she didn't understand. His very sharp quizzical eyes and his sharp nose had always been mysterious. Whether he was making jokes or telling her about Lundine life, Nobby had always kept her guessing, which was what made him such an interesting friend to have.

Now she saw something in his face which was all too easy to understand. She saw simple fear. She saw what she felt herself (if she was honest) most of the time she was out of the cage. She saw nothing but the fear. All the jokes, all the fun, all the enjoyment of food or their hide-and-seek games together… they had just vanished. The fear was the only thing that was real any more. And the fear she saw in her friend's face was something that took over and coloured everything that followed.

The Terror changed everything. Furball could feel Nobby's fear spreading so it would very quickly engulf all of them.

All of a sudden, Mokey Moke appeared and came to the edge of the tray-trap. She called out Nobby's name, but after this they stopped using words. Nobby called to his mother, and his mother called back in a high-pitched wail of grief. That was all that was real.

It is impossible to say how long it lasted. Several of the Rivals came out of the hole and clustered around Mokey Moke. She tried to push them away to keep them from Nobby's fate on the sticky-trap. Buster was probably there too. When Furball tried to remember it afterwards the details became muddled.

Time changed. Hamsters and mice do not think about time in the way humans do, but even a human wouldn't have known if a few seconds or a few hours had passed.

They were all frozen in their fear and caught up in Nobby's agony.

The fear was not over. It was only just beginning. Because, as they all stood there, horrified by Nobby's plight, he called to them – *ooms, ooms*. All of them, including Furball, shrank back into the shadows under the dresser. A large pair of naked oom feet and the flapping legs of some pyjama trousers became visible. The feet came nearer to the dresser, and nearer and nearer…

They heard the oom make groaning and swearing noises. Then his great hand came down to the floor. His large stubby fingers, each one of them large enough to pick up a moke, reached towards the sticky-tray. There was more roaring and cursing. Then two of the large fingers reached towards Nobby himself and tried to pull him off the sticky-tray. But the trap just lifted with the moke, so Nobby screamed even louder and the oom dropped the trap. Next, the fingers tried to push Nobby, but nothing would budge his greyish-pink feet, and the more the fingers tried to move him, the greater the moke's pain.

Then the oom left the kitchen. They could hear crashing and banging and he opened the back door into the yard. The oom came blundering back into the kitchen and they saw its great fingers lifting Nobby and the trap into the air. The oom was carrying Nobby in his trap out into the yard.

When they talked about it afterwards they had different memories about what he had called to them as the oom took him away. Some said he was just screaming. Some seemed to think he was calling their names. Buster always maintained that his brother had been defiant, shouting cheeky comments to the end, 'Ooms stink, mokes rock,' was Buster's version. Furball didn't like talking about that moment. All the same, she could have sworn that when he was lifted up on his trap, Nobby looked down and said, 'Wotcha, Furba! Wotcha!'

While the oom was in the backyard, the younger newborn mokes, the Rivals, clustered around Mokey Moke. Some wanted to snuggle near their mother. Others, already growing up into true mokes, despite such a short time in the world, couldn't resist larking about, elbowing one another, squeaking, dancing in circles.

There was a shelf near the kitchen window with plants on it. Furball and Buster climbed on to it. They could see the yard from here. They could see the oom. It was Kitty's dad. In one hand he carried a plastic bag. In the other hand he was holding a garden rake. The trap, with Nobby stuck to it, was on the paving near the back door. They saw the rake being lifted up, and they saw it come down – once, twice and then again.

In that moment, Furball could have been frozen to the spot with terror. It was almost as if the shelf where they stood was a sticky-trap and her feet would not move. But, with a squeal nearly as loud as Nobby's had been when he was trapped, Buster gave a cry that united all of them. It was a cry of defiance against the ooms and it was a cry to rally all the mokes into retreat.

It was so loud and so powerful that even the tiny mokes who had been larking about near the dresser were summoned into action.

Buster, still squeaking and shrieking, had become their war leader. In many great struggles there comes a moment to retreat. There was nothing they could do to rescue Nobby, and there was nothing they could do to defeat the power of the oom and his garden rake. No thought, exactly – no thought, that is, in the sense of a plan what to do next, occupied the mind either of Mokey Moke or of Buster. But when Buster had reached the ground, he ran back under the dresser into the comforting darkness and all the mokes ran with him. Furball followed. They had not got under the dresser a moment too soon; the oom had come back into the kitchen. And there was not much doubt he wanted to kill more of them. Furball thought she heard him calling her oom name – *Chum! Chum!* She thought of Nobby's bravery on the trap. She thought of what he had told her about old Murphy, the last hamster, and how the ooms had put him into the damp mud of the backyard. And she ran with the mokes.

They did not run this time towards the backyard. Maybe some instinct kept them from running past the scene of Nobby's last heroic minutes. They did not run, either, down the old, familiar, short, dusty passage to the nests and dustbowls under the stairs. They ran forwards instead in the direction of the front of the house. They were behind the kitchen wall. Then, as they ran breathlessly through the dark, and not knowing where they were going, they blundered over bricks, rubble and soot. They came through what felt like a sooty cave, which was an old chimney flue. They ran and ran. At one point they came out of a hole and found themselves in an oom-room. There were large white mats or pieces of carpet over the floor. Two of the Rivals ran about on top of these, thinking they were a game, but Mokey Moke squealed at them that the mats were almost certainly a trap and they should come back inside the wall. Back in the darkness, through a small hole in the floorboards, they ran on and on. There were nine of them – Mokey Moke, Buster, four Rivals and some of the older mokes. And there was their friend Furball the hamster.

As they ran forward now, the dryness and the dustiness changed – first from dampness and then to soaking wet. They had come into the little paved area at the front of the basement, and were running round the outside of some large plastic containers which rose, great

black towers, above their backs. It felt even more terrifying, to be exposed like this to the open air.

'Looking for breakfast?'

A huge grey and white fevva was calling to them in long, sad, gulping cries. Its grey wings were huge. Its big orange-yellow hooked beak was far larger than a moke, and it swooped down into the area and picked up one of the Rivals as if it were a crumb. The little moke was carried up into the air as the fevva – a seagull – flapped away into the trees in the street.

'On! On!' called Buster.

'Hide – oh hide – oh, take care, my poor little mokes,' cried Mokey Moke.

And Furball followed them as they scuttered under the door of an old coal vault, and into the shadows once again.

'You must stay near us,' said Buster. 'Look what happened to im.'

Some of the younger Rivals had not even seen the fevva taking their brother into the sky – it had all happened so quickly. Those who had seen it were reduced to an even wilder state of panic. So it was that when the group of mokes were inside once more, many of them, even the older ones, nuzzled against the soft fur of Furball for comfort, because she was so much larger, and plumper and softer than they were. She herself was quivering with fear. She wanted now, more than anything, to be back in her cage, waiting for the Giant to come and pick her up and stroke her, and feed her seeds and speak to her in her Chum voice. But instead she was in a damp, smelly vault with the mokes.

And, as if she were reading Furball's thoughts, or almost reading them, Mokey Moke said, 'An' I'll tell you what that pong is 'n all.'

'No mistakin' that,' said one of the older mokes.

Furball later picked up the fact that his name was Uncle Sid. He was the least playful moke she had ever met, always willing to look on the dark side of life and always negative, even on those rare occasions (rare for mokes, that is) when things went well. 'Could only be one fing, vat pong.'

'Maybe they gorn,' said Mokey Moke.

Furball, who was quite good at moke language by now, and understood well over half of what they said, replied, 'Maybe who's gone? Gone where?'

'Maybe the *narks* is gorn,' said Mokey Moke.

'Narks?'

Nobby had once told her about narks, with their sharp teeth and foul smell, and long worm-like tails, but she had forgotten this.

'I reckon we've walked slap bang into the middla of narks' lair,' said Uncle Sid.

'Oh, don't, Sid – don't say it,' said another moke.

And the five remaining Rivals all squeaked – *Don't, don't, don't.*

And then, through the darkness, terrible and loud, there came a raucous laugh.

'Reckon you come inta *narks'* lair, didya?'

Out of the shadows stepped a huge brown nark. It looked – first at the young Rivals, and then at Furball.

'Wot in ve nima charity is yew?' it spat.

Furball stammered out, 'Ham– ham –'

'Vats a goodun – am! Am sandwich more like. Muvva!' the nark called.

From the darkness came an even more raucous, even coarser voice. 'Wot izzit, Ray-*mond*?' it asked.

'Only gotta ruddy *torkin* am sandwich, enn-eye?'

'Yew wot?'

Out of the gloaming the other animals saw another nark stepping, even larger, and even coarser, even browner, even smellier than the one who called her Mother. To her thick brown fur there clung moisture. It looked as if she had been paddling or rolling in something really nasty, and the smell was terrible.

'Sez it's am.'

'Wot does?'

'Vat.'

The son nark, by the name of Ray-*mond*, nodded his head. The mother nark, dragging her thick moist worm of a tail approached Furball and against the hamster's pink, delicate quivering nose she shoved her pointy, smelly nark-nose and opened her nark-mouth and bared her brown nark-teeth.

'Wot in the name of bleedin ek is vat?' asked the mother nark.

'Sez its am.' Ray-*mond* really liked this joke. He gave a hoarse chuckle every time he repeated it.

'Well,' said the mother nark with a truly evil leer, 'If it sez its *am*, we all know what we does with *am*. Eh? Eh?'

As she said this, Furball could smell her putrid breath and nark-spit drenched her face. The nark turned and spoke to her son. 'What would you say, son, that we should do ter noice juicy sloicer am, eh?'

'Sez its am,' laughed Ray-*mond* in return.

CHAPTER TWENTY

Little Sooty Footprints

'Have some tea,' said Kitty's dad.

'What time is it?' asked Mum.

'Five to seven.'

Kitty's mum yawned and answered, 'Oh, what a night.'

When he placed a mug of tea on her bedside table, she sat up and said, 'Peter? What's the matter?'

He sighed, a very long drawn-out sigh.

'You're trembling. You're pale. It's Chum, isn't it? Chum got caught in the trap!'

'It's not Chum,' said Kitty's dad.

'Well then?'

'But there was one trap still left down.'

He was very careful *not* to say, '*there was still one trap which* you *had left down,*' but she still felt bad about it and snapped at him. 'Peter, I asked you to go downstairs and check.'

He was silent for a while and sipped at his mug of tea. 'It was *awful.* There was a mouse caught in that *thing.*'

'That's why I put it there.'

'Allie, it was *stuck* there.'

'That's the idea of the traps.'

'It was squeaking and squawking in terror.'

'You haven't just *left* it there?'

'Its eyes looked up into mine. They were no different from Chum's eyes. I just couldn't help thinking – supposing it *had* been Chum caught in the trap.'

'I'm so glad it wasn't. What did you do to the little brute? Drown it?'

'Allie, it was screaming and struggling. I just didn't know what to do. At first I tried to get it off the trap.'

'You mean, let the smelly thing *go*?'

'But he was stuck fast. So I just wanted to end its suffering as soon as possible. I took it in the garden – it was terrible.'

'How did you do it?'

Kitty's dad groaned. 'I hit him with a rake a few times. Then I poured water over the body from the watering can – just to make sure. He'd have drowned then. Then I wrapped him in a plastic bag and put him in the dustbin.'

'At least you're not asking us to have a funeral.'

'You'd have felt the same if you'd found him. I just had this sense when he looked up into my face that he was a fellow creature; that I had no right to take his life.'

Mum smiled at him. 'Are you a man,' she asked, 'or a mouse?'

They decided not to tell Kitty about the mouse. It was upsetting enough that Chum had, yet again, gone missing. They really didn't need to tell Kitty about the sticky-traps, and – as they saw it – the hamster's lucky escape.

'Suppose it had been Chum caught in that thing? I couldn't have killed her –'

'You'd have had to.'

'Alex, we must find a different solution to the mouse problem.'

Kitty's mum was a practical person, and she knew that there were only three possible 'solutions to the mouse problem'. The first solution was to do nothing. There are seven million people in London and probably getting on for thirty million mice. These mice are going to live somewhere, and the likeliest place for them to choose is within reach of human houses, so they could eat the food that people hoard, store, drop or throw away. Everywhere you looked in London there were mice. In the underground railway stations mice leaped across the electrified rails and hopped about the platforms, picking up crusts of bread dropped from sandwiches, gnawing on apple cores, chewing pieces of paper. On street corners and in gutters, indoors and out of doors, there were mice.

She knew that she couldn't change this. But she didn't want mice in *her* house. The mice were dirty and smelly and they made a mess. And that same morning she found mayhem everywhere: half-chewed vegetables on the larder floor, and a whole packet of biscuits, broken and half-chewed, on the kitchen floor.

Worse than this, when she went into her office at the front of the house, she found little footprints all over a document which she had just printed out from her computer.

Clearly she had to do *something*, so option number one, doing nothing, was no use. There were only two alternatives: either to kill the mice, or to stop them getting in. Killing them upset everybody and she worried about the hamster. She would just have to make sure the house itself was mouseproof: to block up all the holes, cracks and cavities which let them in.

Kitty's mum went over every inch of the house before she called in Ted, her favourite builder.

And so, a day or two after Kitty's dad had found the mouse in the sticky-trap, Mum took Ted on the tour. They started in the small paved garden at the back of the house. She pointed to holes in the brickwork through which it was possible to imagine mice squeezing. They examined drainage holes and ventilation shafts. Once inside, they peered at the holes through which pipework burst into plastering. They looked in the larder, and at the various holes and cracks under the stairs. Then they went to the kitchen, and lay under the sink. They moved back the dresser. There were many intakes of breath here.

'I reckon *this* is one of the places they've been using. Look here,' said Ted.

Kitty's mum fetched a dustpan and brush to sweep up crumbs and – she couldn't help noting – two sorts of droppings. The tiny pellets left by the mice and the slightly larger little turds usually found in the hamster cage.

'That's not all,' she said. And she led the builder to her small basement office at the front of the house. 'Somehow they got in here. Look at this!'

She held up her document, covered with little sooty pawprints. And this time she noted there were *two* sorts of pawprints – some tiny ones, which must be from the mice, and some which were a bit bigger, more the size of a hamster's. She couldn't be sure of this, and the thought slipped out of her mind while Ted, lying on the floor beneath the window, looked at the skirting board under the radiator.

Then Ted went with a torch into the area at the front of the house to look round the coal vaults. These searches were a bit less thorough, but when he turned to Kitty's mum he had a funny expression on his face.

'I don't want to worry you,' he said, 'but I think I just seen a rat scurrying out of there.'

CHAPTER TWENTY-ONE

Guzzling Narks

'Lucky escape,' said Mokey Moke.

They had run through the house, and beyond the area. In an old coal vault near the dustbins, they had met the two narks, Ray-*mond* and his mother. None of them wanted to hang around to see if he and his mother were joking when they spoke as if Furball was a ham sandwich. They had scarpered. At one end of the coal vault there were holes in the brickwork, leading through to another vault. The narks could follow them but at present it didn't look as if they would. Right now the mokes needed to find a part of the vault where they could hide – away from ooms, away from narks, away from the big white fevvas with their huge, sharp, orange beaks.

Mokey Moke could not count. She knew that one of her babies had been eaten by a seagull, and that earlier that day an oom had killed Nobby. But she didn't have any means of knowing whether all the mokes were safe, or how many had followed her and Furball in the stampede to the front of the house and the coal vaults.

Still, Mokey Moke could not look after all the mokes. Even the little Rivals must learn that the rule of life was this: *every moke for isself*.

Furball lay in the darkness. They all kept close together because it was comforting after all they had been through. But they also huddled close because none of them, not even Mokey Moke, had the smallest idea where they were.

Furball, who had lost all sense of direction, said, 'Maybe if we go on we'll reach the backyard and the shed I was telling you about.'

'Yeah, and maybe we'll get eaten by vat snark you was telling me abart an' all.'

'The snark didn't come in the shed,' said Furball.

'I'm sure that, once we were settled there, the Giant would bring us food.'

'Yeah, oom food – vat's all we need,' said Mokey Moke in the darkness. 'Floor-food more like, or food in the ole snapper – like Aunty Flo.'

'I'm sure the Giant means us no harm,' persisted Furball. 'If she knew where we were, she *would* bring us food, she would.'

'Yeah, an' you thought vat sticky-trap were a trampoline an all,' said Mokey Moke, with a sigh.

They became very hungry in the darkness of the vault. Furball emptied her pouch and shared the remains of biscuit, pearl barley and other delicacies stored there, but these didn't go far among a gang of hungry mokes. Buster ran under the door of the vault and found that it led to the paved outside area. The dustbins had lately been emptied, and one of the bin bags had burst, dropping a few very tasty-looking potato peelings.

There was rejoicing among the mokes when Buster came into the vault bearing this very welcome treasure. He put down the first bit of potato peel and Furball immediately volunteered to come with him to the basement area to retrieve some more.

'You can pouch more than I can carry, Furball, ole girl,' he agreed.

But when they reached the area, they were not alone. Furball had no sooner picked up some potato peel when she heard a voice – a familiar voice.

'Well, well, well – if it ain't the am. The am sandwich,' said the mother nark. 'Ray-*mond* – we ave company.'

'Wot did you think you woz doin?' Ray-*mond* asked Furball.

'I was coming to fetch some potato peelings,' said Furball with artless truthfulness.

'Oh, you woz, woz yer?'

'I heard that some peelings had been dropped,' said Furball.

'And the am sandwich thought to issel – oi'd *loik* summa vat vere per-tater.'

'Yes,' said Furball. It pleased her that the narks were friendlier than they had been when she first met them.

'So you thought you'd jus' come and eat the per-tater – did yer, am sandwich?'

'Just some of it,' said Furball truthfully. 'The rest, I thought I would share with my friends.'

'Jus' share it, did yer, *sandwich*?'

'That is correct,' said Furball, her voice now trembling a little. Although the narks were surely trying to be friendly, there was something – well, just a little frightening about the way they bared their teeth at her.

'And so –' the mother nark laughed in a way which even Furball, with her desire to think the best of others, thought was a little unpleasant, 'And so, which friends woz yer a-goin ter share vat pertikler pertater wiv, if you don't mind my askin'?'

'I rather thought,' said Furball, trembling, 'of sharing it with the Rivals, who are too young to –'

But she wasn't able to finish. Ray-*mond* jumped towards her and hit her vigorously on the side of the head. She fell, and felt a sharp pain as he bit her in the back and the tail. She lay on her side quivering as he brought his cruel, smelly face close to hers.

'Wotcha *meant* ter say, am *sandwich*, woz that you woz goin' er share yer pertater wiv Ray-*mond* and wiv iz dear ole mother.'

'I really…'

Perhaps it wasn't very safe to explain to Ray-*mond* what she'd meant. Perhaps with Ray-*mond* it was safer to say nothing.

'Vat woz wotcha menter say, am.'

Furball wasn't strong enough to reply. She wished she could explain the true facts to the nark. Although he seemed stupid (not that she wished to be unkind), surely he'd understand if she explained that the Rivals were very small and very hungry, and so was their mother, and she'd been finding food for *them*?

But Ray-*mond* was still talking.

'You tell it – our Ray-*mond*,' said its mother through her sharp orangey-brown teeth. 'Tell the little bleeder.'

'Taters, or rather as I should say since you're so lah de bleedin' da – per-taters – isn't am's, isn't no *sandwich*'s, isn't the *sandwich*'s little friends, the mokes. Taters is narks'. Wot is taters?'

'I – I –' Furball was now speechless with fear.

And while Ray-*mond* repeated his question, 'Wot iz taters?' his mother urged him on with, 'You tell it, Ray-*mond*.'

'Taters is narks'.' He had advanced on Furball and cuffed her round the head with a sharp claw. 'What is taters?'

'N-n-narks,' Furball managed to say.

'And if you woz ter find, let us say, a nice chicken bone – ooz would that be?'

'Narks'?' Furball ventured.

'Too right it ud be narks'. An apple core? A sosij?'

'Narks'?'

'Old cakes? Rotten cabbage? Remains of a lamb

chop wot some wasteful oom az gorn and thrown art? Any views as to rightful ownership?'

Furball didn't know what he was talking about, but she felt it was safer to whimper, 'Narks'?'

'Too right it's narks'. And just in case any on yer – *any* on that *putrid* little gang on yer in there *thinks* of eating *anything*, I repeats, *anything* out near these ere bins – you'll ave the narks to answer to.'

'You tell it, Ray-*mond*,' echoed his mother.

'And next time, *am sandwich*, I won't just tell you, nice and gentle, like I'm telling yer now. Yer know what I'll do?'

'You tell it, Ray-*mond*.'

Furball shook her head in acknowledgement that she had no idea what Ray-*mond* would do were he to find either the hamster or the mokes daring to satisfy their hunger on dustbin rubbish.

'Next time, I'll tear you, am sandwich. Next time, there'll be a bit o' am sandwich ere and a bit o' am sandwich there, only *which* bits no one will be able ter rightly say. Gottit?'

Furball had got it. Luckily, as she scurried away

from the nark to the comparative safety of the vault, she had some potato peel in her pouch. But when that had run out – where would she and the mokes find food to keep them alive?

CHAPTER TWENTY-TWO

Mouse-Proof House

About a week later, Ted rang up to say that the job he was working on had been cancelled, and that he was now free to start work on Mum's grand project: making the house mouseproof. Both Dad and Kitty had groaned slightly when they realised how thorough Mum had been in her plans. They all liked Ted. He had done most of the building and decorating work for them for as long as Kitty could remember. Kitty and her dad had hoped that Ted would just do a little bit of patching and tinkering – a dub of Polyfilla here, a bit of new skirting board there.

Mum had very different ideas. The whole of the basement in their house was to have a thorough makeover. Every bit was to be overhauled, including Mum's little study at the front, and the kitchen-dining room at the back. She would have a new floor installed so the mice couldn't nip in and out through holes in the old floorboards. All holes in the walls were to be patched and sealed. Various pipes running in and out of the house through the brickwork were to be wedged round with thick coatings of cement so that the little 'beggars' – almost the word Mum used – could not wriggle in that way.

While Ted was about it, Mum had decided he should clear out the old coal vaults at the front of the house.

'I'm *not* going to let myself be beaten,' said Mum, 'by a bunch of little *vermin.*'

When she said it, at supper one evening, to prepare Dad and Kitty for the start of the works, a look of sadness suddenly passed over her face, and there was a silence at the table. They were all thinking of Chum. She had been missing over a week and it seemed very unlikely that they would ever see her again.

They had all, in fact, given themselves up to the

idea that she was dead.

When Murphy had died, it had been very sad, but not as sad as this. Kitty thought she knew one of the reasons for this. They'd got used to the idea of his being dead because they could see his dead body. They had each in turn held the poor, still little handful of fur, and said goodbye to him before they buried him in the flowerbed at the back of the house. They could say goodbye properly.

Kitty had not said goodbye to Chum. Of course, she knew that her hamster was almost certainly dead. She had never been lost for as long as this. And building work was about to begin, which would make it impossible to find her if she had burrowed under a floorboard or behind the kitchen dresser. And yet… and yet… Because she had not actually seen Chum's dead body, Kitty found it impossible not to go on hoping. Hoping that her little Chum's pink nose would come snuffling out of the skirting board, or from the larder, or from a place by the coats and shoes where she liked to hide. On some mornings, Kitty woke up and forgot Chum had gone, and she would look – with aching longing – at the empty cage. And on some evenings, Kitty would close her eyes after she had gone to bed and just *wish* – wish that she could wake up in the morning and find that it had all been a bad dream, and that Chum was back with them again. It was this hope, this unstoppable hope, which made Chum's disappearance so much harder to bear than if they had actually seen her dead.

But once the building work began, the hope seemed more and more unrealistic. Mum meant business. She was determined to make it impossible for mice to come in. And if there were no holes for mice to get through, it was hard to see how Chum could ever get back – if she was alive, which Kitty knew she wasn't. And yet. And yet.

'You will *ask* Ted,' Kitty persisted, 'to look out for Chum? To be – well, to be *careful*?'

When Mum mentioned to Ted that there was an outside chance, a very, very remote possibility, that there was a hamster at large somewhere or other, he smiled.

'I'll do my best for you, Alex – but it'd be like finding a needle in a haystack, really. I mean, 'e could be in the vaults out the front. 'E could be behind the cooker, behind the fridge. 'E could…'

'*She*,' blurted out Mum sadly. '*She* could. *She*, not he. But we don't think…'

'Well, I mean, I don't want to depress you, but 'e wouldn't stand a chance. Not really. A cat could 'ave got 'im on 's first hour out. Really.'

'Her,' said Mum, who hated what Ted was saying. 'A cat could have got *her*.'

Ted brought a Polish worker with him. Bogdán – this was the Polish worker's name – did not have more than a few sentences of English. Ted certainly had no Polish, and though Alex looked up *rat* and *mouse* in a Russian dictionary which Dad had bought once in a car-boot sale (didn't Polish have a very similar vocabulary to Russian?), they didn't have a word for *hamster*. Not in their dictionary anyway. Peter said that the Russians had a letter G where English-speakers had the letter H. For instance, they spoke about Shakespeare's play *Gamlet*. One morning, before setting off to work, Peter tried to say to Bogdán, 'If you see gamster – very good. Save gamster. If you see *rat* – very bad – kill rat.'

'I'm afraid you're getting him in a muddle there,' laughed Ted.

Kitty wished Dad had not started this stupid conversation with Ted and Bogdán. She knew that Ted was a nice man, but she couldn't help hating him when he *laughed* about her lost hamster. He made it worse when he said, 'No. *Really*. It's sad for kids. When they lose their pets. *Really*.'

Ted and Bogdán started with a complete clear-out of the coal vaults. Bogdán saw a rat and tried to chase it, but he missed. Neither of them saw a hamster, but as Ted remarked to Mum one day, 'A little pet like that – quite frankly, Alex, it could have been squashed without one knowing. *Really*. I mean, you've got so much stuff piled up in those vaults, you've got your deckchairs, your two old beds in there, you've got –'

'I don't know how we've managed to collect so much *rubbish* over the years,' said Mum. She stopped her own work in the downstairs office and put on blue overalls to sort out objects to keep, things to be sold, and things to be thrown away.

This tidying and cleaning and sorting, and the work

on the empty vaults which followed, took much longer than Ted had expected.

'I wanted to help them clear out the vaults,' Mum explained to Dad when they were alone together. 'I just *hoped*. I thought Chum might have got in there somehow.'

'It doesn't seem very likely,' said Dad.

'I know she's probably stuck somewhere in the kitchen. I know when they take up the kitchen floor they'll probably...' She couldn't quite bring herself to say, *They will find Chum's dead body.*

'She's almost certainly stuck somewhere in the kitchen,' said Dad sadly. 'Behind the fridge, behind the dishwasher – anywhere.'

At breakfast, Kitty asked, 'Mum, how much longer is this going on?'

The men hadn't finished the vaults at the front, but they had somehow also made the downstairs part of the house unliveable. In every corner there seemed to be bundles of grey, dusty sheets spattered with white paint; chrome folding stepladders, spattered with pink plaster; endless tools, chalky and paint-spattered, boxes of screws, paint tins, bags of dried plaster. Ted had assured Mum that the work would be done with the minimum of disruption. Already, her downstairs study was draped with plaster-coated sheets of cellophane. The downstairs hall was the same. No one could go in the larder without kicking paint pots or buckets, and the kitchen itself was filling up with Ted's clutter.

'It will be over in a few days,' said Mum. 'In a couple of weeks we'll have forgotten all the chaos and everything will be lovely. We'll have two clean new storerooms instead of that grotty coal hole. Ted's making my study into a spare bedroom with a shower while I've moved all my stuff up to the spare bedroom upstairs. And we'll have a new kitchen, and –'

'Then it can't possibly be ready in a few days,' said Kitty. 'Why do builders say a few days when they mean a few weeks?'

'Because they want to please,' said Dad.

'Because they hope what they say is true,' said Mum. 'And that's not quite the same as lying.'

'The effect's the same,' said Kitty.

The breakfast cereal she was eating tasted of plaster dust.

They endured it for a few more days and then they admitted defeat. Their friends the Blackstones kindly asked them to stay until the work was completed.

Kitty went to school with Emma Blackstone, who was her age, and with Emma's brother Tim, who was two years younger. Kitty's heart sank when Mum told her they would be staying with the Blackstones. It wasn't that she disliked them. But she knew she'd be sharing a bedroom with Emma. And that would mean sharing a bedroom with Radish, Emma's rather unloved hamster.

Sure enough, as they lay there in the dark, chatting about their school day and laughing about their teachers, Kitty found herself caught in mid-giggle with a stab of grief. Because Emma didn't clean Radish's cage as often as she should, there was a strong hamster smell in the bedroom. Kitty could hear the little fellow climbing up the side of his cage, and the sound of hamster claws on cage wire painfully reminded her of Chum.

Emma continued to giggle and prattle in the dark. 'And then she went, like – I *so* didn't take your gym bag, and I was like, *Ha–nah*, I *saw* you take it and then Miss Macleod? And, like, it was *so-o-o* unfair, she came up and she went – What are you two doing in the locker room? Aren't you like…?'

And Kitty was silent, listening to Radish scuttling about in his cage.

'Kitty? Are you asleep already?' asked Emma.

Kitty said nothing, but could feel tears on her cheeks.

CHAPTER TWENTY-THREE

Every Moke for Isself

Buster and one of the Rivals, called Frankie-boy, were
waiting anxiously in the 'safe' vault to see if Ray-*mond*
and his mother had fallen asleep. The two narks had
eaten enough to send anyone to sleep. They
knew they were being watched,
because as they gorged on a
chicken leg, a hunk of bread
with blue mould on
it, 'Just the way my
Ray-*mond* likes
it' – and a fish's
head, they made
pointed remarks.

'I bet as there's *some* little mokes wot should never ave bin born wot would kill fer a bit of this eer chicking.'

'Ray-*mond* – finish it up, son – yer don't want no mokes eatin' yer nosh.'

'No, Mum –' sounds of slurping and stuffing and chewing, 'only like I say, I bet there's those as ud love to eat as much as we're eatn' *nar* but as isn't goin' to get so much as a morsel, not from me, not from you, not from eether on us.'

The narks' banter and the guzzling seemed to go on for hours, but eventually there was – not silence exactly, but the rather disgusting sound of a pair of satisfied narks settling down to an after-dinner sleep. There were burping, farting, snuffling and snoring sounds as the two smelly creatures curled up into an old rag which they used as bedding.

'When they's properly off, kid – we'll see what we can see, eh?'

'Sure will, Uncle Buster,' squeaked Frankie-boy. The plan was to squeeze under the door of 'their' vault and look for food in the territory forbidden them by the narks, namely the area near the dustbins.

'Cor they snore,' laughed Frankie-boy.

'It might be a bluff,' whispered Buster.

But before he could explain his unlikely theory that both narks were pretending to be asleep, the door of the narks' vault was ripped open and two enormous ooms entered. They seized hold of two old bedsteads leaning against the wall and carried them out to the dustbin area. One of them with gigantic boots almost trod on Ray-*mond*'s nark mother. The old nark squealed with shock and ran. Ray-*mond*, still stupid with sleep and overeating, lumbered after her.

The younger moke, by instinct, gave a high-pitched squeal for his mother, '*Mokey-Mo-o-oke!*'

Buster said, 'Stay close to me, young Frankie-boy.' But their voices were drowned by the thunderous din. The older and the younger moke scampered back under the door of 'their' vault and called the alarm.

'Out – *out* – out now – ooms! Ooms!'

'Where?'

'Never mind where – out – we gotta get *out*! Get the young 'uns – *out*!' Buster was shouting desperately into the darkness.

There was a chaos of chattering moke voices. Everyone who had been shut up in that vault, hiding from the narks, was by now extremely hungry. This made them not only weak, but bleary and sleepy. Some of the mokes were slow to realise they were in danger.

Mokey Moke was wide awake, and trying to rouse her sleepy children. She knew that some of them would die of starvation, but she wanted to save as many as she could. Of the large numbers of mokes who had escaped from the house about a week before, six survived.

'What's going on?' she yelled.

'Sounds like they're pulling whole place to bits,' gasped Buster. 'Got to get – *out*!'

'Take Frankie-boy, Kev, Tone – I'll try and wake up the others.'

'Where shall we run to?'

'Inside again.'

'But –'

'No time for buts, Mokey.'

This exchange took only a few seconds. All a human could have heard would have been two mice squeaking.

'What about Furba?' asked Mokey Moke as they ferried young mice out of the vault to a hiding place behind the dustbins.

'What about her?'

'We can't leave er in vere.'

'Every moke for isscl, Mokey Moke.'

'The narks is in there. Ran into our vault. I could smell em. Even if the ooms leave our vault alone – we can't leave Furba behind. Not on er own in vere wiv the narks.'

'Mokey – it's er or us.'

'No, Buster. It ain't. It's er *and* us.'

Buster looked at his mother. He hoped she wouldn't remember what he'd just said. 'I'll find er,' he said.

'We can't waste too much time, though,' squeaked Mokey Moke.

'Make your bloomin mind up,' he called as he ran back into the dark. It was hard to call out for Furball against the crashing din of the ooms in the next-door vault. Having removed the bedsteads and some boxes and some deckchairs, the ooms were bringing out armfuls of old junk. They were shouting to one another. If the mokes could have understood English they would have heard Ted saying, 'She says we can chuck all this lot in the skip.' And: 'Bloomin' eck – d'yer see that, Bogdán, bloody great *rat.*'

'E gamster?'

'No, it ain't a bloomin' amster – it were a *rat,*' said Ted, before yet more crushing and banging.

Buster ran into the dark. The stench of nark was overwhelming. Every instinct made him want to run – at the smell of the narks and the noise of the ooms. But he knew he must make one last effort to find Furball.

He wasn't exactly looking. It was too dark in there to focus his eyes. He ran this way and that, hoping to find her, and realising that he almost certainly never would. At one point, when he was in the depths of the vault, the smell of nark became overwhelming. Much too late, he realised he was almost face to face with stinking Ray-*mond.*

'Wot d'you want, moke – want ter get us all killed, do yer?'

Buster didn't answer. He ran off, and could hear the nark mother and Ray-*mond* still talking in the smelly shadows.

It was no good. He had tried his best. He would never find Furball. What would he say to Mokey Moke? There was nothing he *could* say.

He left the vault *just* in time. The enormous plaster-caked boots of one of the ooms came crunching in, and Buster managed to slip between his trouser legs without being noticed. A grim pleasure at thinking of the fate which would befall the narks was clouded by grief for the friend they had lost. She'd been a good friend to the mokes, Furball had. *Chum* was what the ooms called her. Nobby had told Buster that a chum was what she had been – sharing her food, pouching nosh and squeezing with it behind the skirting board to feed Mokey Moke when she was having the Rivals. One of the best, old Furball.

He was just having these sad thoughts as he scuttled across the area yard towards the dustbins, when he came face to face with the curranty eyes and excited expression of the hamster.

'Oh, Buster! I was coming back to rescue you,' she said.

'*You* were coming to rescue *me* – that's a larf! I was coming –'

'I've found some food. Come quickly.'

On a packing case just inside the door of the house, Furball had found a packet containing soft white bread and cheese. She had scuttled back to tell Mokey Moke and the younger mokes. Then she had run back to fetch Buster, who now found something a bit like a party in progress. The little mokes were calling out, 'Cheese! Cheese! Cheese!'

And Mokey Moke was saying, between mouthfuls, 'Eat all you can, mokes, it might be the last meal we all ave for a long while.'

'But – Furba – Furball, ole mate! Furba – my *chum* – where woz yer?'

'I heard the ooms coming,' explained Furball, 'and I thought it might be the Giant coming to put out our food. So I ran indoors to have a look. When I saw that she had put down enough bread and cheese for all of us, I ran back to tell Mokey Moke while two of the larger ooms were moving furniture.'

'Good old Furba! You really think the Giant put out this food – for *us*?'

'For all of us, Buster,' said Furball earnestly. 'I told you she wouldn't desert us.'

She found it difficult to see why this remark made all the mokes laugh so heartily. But she was glad to please them and even more glad that her faith in the Giant had been justified. There was so much bread and cheese here in the greaseproof-paper packet that even seven hungry mokes and a hungry hamster couldn't possibly eat it all in one meal. No doubt the Giant meant her to pouch as much as possible and to store at least part of it in some safe place, while the others continued enjoying the meal.

'The question is,' Mokey Moke was saying, 'where do we go from ere? We obviously can't go back out front. But the ooms is everywhere today and we can't stay ere eating their grub –'

'The Giant's grub,' corrected Furball.

But as often happened when mokes were standing round wondering what to do next, the decision was taken out of their hands. The younger Rivals squealed, '*Ooms, ooms,*' and the whole party – Furball by now a hammer-headed shark with her pouches full of bread and cheese – ran for the open fireplace. By the time the ooms had crashed noisily back into the room, all of them were hidden from view.

CHAPTER TWENTY-FOUR

A Gap in the Skirting Board

'Haven't we got enough on our plate,' asked Kitty's mum, 'without adding Emma's hamster to our list of worries?'

'*Mu-er-um*. It's just for the weekend – while Emma goes to a family wedding.'

'I know you,' said Mum. 'It will be just for the weekend, and then just for the little bleeder's lifetime – Rubbish, or whatever she's called.'

'Radish. And it's a he.'

'Well, I'm not so sure. Ted hasn't even finished his work yet. I must say, he is taking his time.'

'I really hate sharing a bedroom with Emma,' Kitty said.

'We hear you chattering late into the night,' said Mum.

'I'd still rather be alone.'

'Yes,' said Dad, 'I'll be glad to be in our own home again – even though it's incredibly kind of Lucy and Richard to have us to stay so long.'

'I want to be home too,' said Mum.

So – they went home. And the following weekend, when Emma and her family went to a family wedding, they agreed to look after her hamster, Radish. It was, as Dad said, the very least they could do, to have a hamster to stay for two or three nights, when the hamster's owners had had them to stay for over two weeks.

Ted was justly proud of his work. He didn't tell Kitty's mum that behind the dresser there was a gap of two inches in the skirting board. Ted had measured the space in feet and inches. Bogdán had measured it in centimetres. When they brought the wood back from the timber yard they were about two inches short. But as Ted said to Bogdán – not that the smiling Pole understood him –'What the eye does not see, the heart does not grieve over.'

Mum showed Dad and Kitty round the new basement with great pride. It was almost as if she was showing it to visitors, or even to people who might buy it from her.

'Notice the tiled kitchen floor,' she said, 'going right up to the skirting boards all round the room. Nowhere for our little friends to wriggle through. And then *here*' – she flung open the larder door – 'you'll find a nice clean larder. We have our bags of flour, our cereal packets, our biscuits – no way our friends will get in *here*.'

'What about there?' asked Dad, pointing to a little gap in the wall by the very top shelf.

'I think it's an air vent,' said Mum. 'It's an air vent. And on the top shelf. I don't see a little mouse climbing all the way up there. They aren't *flying* mice.'

'And then in *here*,' said Mum, leading to the front of the house, where her study had once been, 'is a nice little spare bedroom.'

'And you've got your power-shower,' said Ted proudly. 'And then, out the front, lovely clean vaults, plenty of storage space.'

'And no R.A.T.S,' said Dad.

'Some people,' said Kitty, 'are E.L.E.V.E.N. and can S.P.E.L.L.'

'You wonder where they go, don't you,' mused Dad. He turned to Ted. 'I mean, you didn't find anything when you were clearing out, did you?'

'Any dead 'uns?' asked Ted.

Dad flinched at the directness of Ted's language. The builder said, 'No – didn't see a trace of 'em. Not a trace.'

It was, indeed, good to be home. All three of them recognised that it had been kind of Emma's family to let them stay for such a long time. But they wanted to be in their own beds at night, and by day, they wanted to be among their own books, their own belongings.

It wasn't the most restful of Saturday mornings for Kitty. She had wanted to spend it doing absolutely nothing, sitting in the small upstairs living room with the computer, the TV and Radish in his cage. But Ted had still not completely finished his work downstairs. There were occasional hammerings and bangings from the kitchen regions of the house, and shouts to Bogdán. At one point, Mum brought Ted into the living room and they peered up the fireplace. There had been an old gas fire there when Mum and Dad had bought the house. They had removed this because it looked ugly, but although there was now an open fireplace, they didn't burn fires there. They tried it once, as Mum was explaining to Ted, and the upstairs bedroom had filled with smoke.

'Yeah,' said Ted, whose head was now stuck up the chimney, 'you see that. I mean, you had a cracked flue, and the crack could be literally anywhere. *Really*. To be honest with you, short of taking the whole chimney breast down and rebuilding from scratch…' He laughed at the possibility and added, 'really.'

Kitty looked up sharply. For Kitty and her dad, builders' work was a bore and a pain, and they both wanted it finished quickly. So too, of course, did Mum. But Mum also liked giving instructions to builders, and she enjoyed the excitement of new building projects. Kitty would not entirely trust her mother not to set Ted the task of finding the crack in the chimney flue, even if it did mean putting several rooms to ruins in the process.

'And who's that then?' asked Ted in a friendly spirit, smiling down at Radish, who sat, rather shyly quivering on Kitty's lap.

Radish was a very different hamster from Chum. To tell the truth, he was a little bit of a bore. Kitty felt that Emma had done nothing to stimulate her hamster. She hardly ever let the little fellow out of his cage, which wasn't often cleaned. There would have been no question with Radish, as there had been with dear little Chum, of inventing a voice for him, or pretending that he could speak to the Giant or Allie (Mum) or Mister Peter (Dad). Radish just sat there, quivering. On occasion, he would run about the tubes in his cage. For the rest of the time, he either ate or slept.

'You'll have been glad to have got *him* back then,' said Ted pleasantly.

Kitty just smiled and nodded. It was too complicated to explain that this was *not* her lost hamster, and that she was just looking after Radish for the weekend.

'Where d'you find him then?'

'Well,' began Kitty, 'he's not exactly…'

'Under the floorboards?' asked Ted. 'In the airing-cupboard?'

'Sort of,' said Kitty.

'*Really?*'

Ted and Mum were making their progress upstairs. While Mum had Ted in the house, there was a whole shopping list of small tasks which she wanted him to work on either now or at a future date. When she mentioned the guttering, Ted laughed and said, 'Some of the jobs I done. And animals. *Really*. I worked on a house up in Finchley and there was this kitten. Well, I'd taken up the floorboards to see to the wiring – it was in a terrible state. Dear, oh, dear. We fixed it all up, and we put back the floorboards...'

His merry laughter echoed up the stairs.

Kitty flicked through the channels on TV. The choice was between sport, and the drivel of Saturday-morning children's programmes. She didn't switch off, but the chatter on the screen didn't hold her attention. She was soon much more interested in a game on the laptop. As she clocked up more and more points in the game, her eyes were focused ever more fixedly on the screen, away from the little hamster who had jumped off her lap and who, very tentatively, was pitter-pattering across the sofa.

CHAPTER TWENTY-FIVE

Up the Chimblee

It was a bit of a nuisance, clambering all the way down the chimney when they needed more supplies of food, but in general, as they all agreed, it was the best berth yet. There was quite a gang of them – Uncle Sid, Buster, Mokey Moke, Frankie-boy, Kev and others, not to mention their chum, Furball.

Furball was more skilful than the mokes at climbing the chimney. It took her only about thirty seconds to leave their comfortable fluffy nest behind the living-room fireplace and come out of the spacious doorway which – Furball felt sure – the Giant had had built into the kitchen. From there, she and her friends had foraged quite enough food to live on, though they were sometimes became thirsty. There had been a wonderful day when the building-ooms had left out for them a paper packet full of fried potatoes. But even on sparser days there had been crumbs, crusts, an old chicken bone to drag back under the dresser. The terrifying banging noises of the ooms died down. And then, one glad day, Buster brought the news that the ooms were restocking the larder.

Furball spent part of her time helping Buster to forage for food, and part of the time helping Mokey Moke, who was becoming surprisingly fat again, even though none of them were greedy like the narks. Furball didn't like to make comments about her friend's change in weight, but Buster did. 'Mum's filled art agin now she's up the duff.'

It was all most mysterious. But interesting. As were the tales which Buster or Uncle Sid told the Rivals as they sat round in the evening after their crust of bread or piece of apple core. Furball could listen forever as the mokes told of their adventures, or celebrated the brave deeds of mokes who had perished. To the stories of Aunt Flo and the snapper, or poor old Uncle Barney and the floor-food there would now be added the tale of Nobby and the glue-tray, or the time one of the Rivals was grabbed by a fevva 'wot swooped out of a clear sky'.

Furball couldn't hope to rival such heroic sagas, but the younger Rivals, in particular, loved to be told of the time she found a chicken pie in the kitchen. In fact, even the older mokes preferred the chicken-pie story to the stories of blood and gore.

Buster's view was that any of the food put out in the larder was likely to be a trap. This opinion was shared by the ever-gloomy Uncle Sid. The pessimistic Sid was also the only moke to realise that they were nesting in a chimney. As far as Furball and her other moke friends were concerned, it was just a slightly sooty bit of wall, highly convenient for nipping in and out of – especially now the ooms were back in the house. The living room was used more and more. Biscuits were eaten there; even buns with raisins. All good pickings.

For Uncle Sid, though, things looked different. 'Yer realise wot ooms use these caves *for*?'

'Nar.'

'Fer smoke. Fer fire. Fer roastin' mokes alive – that's what they're *for*.'

The opinion was greeted with unbelief.

From the younger mokes there was many a *Never!* and *Gid aw-eye!* at the suggestion that ooms would deliberately set fire to their present nest. Sid, though, would not be budged in his view. In the last house he'd been in – well, maybe not the last, maybe the one *before* it – there'd been one of them caves. *Chimblee* was their proper name. Nice and snug. Whole family of mokes. Nice and comfy. Easy access to food supplies. Everyfink lovely. Comfy nests on brick ledges just like this one. And then, one day, some heat – you couldn't breathe. *E* – Sid – had had a lucky escape, run down towards the flames, then took a left down a dark passage and out through a skirting board. A few mokes what come with him had also escaped. What happened to the ones who'd run up the chimblee he didn't like to think. Chokin' to death. Chokin.

Mokey Moke told Sid he was an old misery-guts. Even if it was true, she said, they'd cross that bridge when they came to it. For the time being, it was hard to imagine a better place to be. Furball agreed. She wondered if the chimblee was the same as the duff, that mysterious place where Mokey Moke went sometimes. But now was not the moment to ask since, about this time, Mokey Moke was joined by another party of baby mokes – or Rivals. Where they were coming from at such a rate was more than Furball could guess.

The Rivals fed from Mokey for the first day or two but – just as before – this meant that Mokey herself was even more hungry. Furball was only too happy to be Mokey's chum and search for food.

She knew the way so well by now that she even had a name for it: the larder run. Down the dark sooty cave, left, then right, then a wiggle, then down a long very dusty tunnel, over a few bits of broken brick, on towards more fluff, where you began to see a patch of light, and then – the *door* – which (she remained convinced) had been built for her by the Giant.

Once she'd come to the Giant's door, she put out her little pink nose and her whiskers and sniffed for danger. She looked right and left. She looked out for narks, snarls, claws and unfriendly ooms. As she did so, she also still looked out, half hopefully, for the one oom she trusted, the Giant. Furball was not like an oom, so she didn't *miss* the Giant, not exactly. But very nearly. Often, as she scuttled quickly along, she imagined that she was going to be picked up by the Giant. And it never occurred to her to suppose that she wouldn't see the Giant again. Without actually *thinking* about it, she supposed that snuggling under the Giant's shirt was – well, one of the things she did. It would be something that happened again one of these days.

Out of the Giant's door, *sniff, sniff, quiver-whiskers.* Out into the shadows under the dresser. A quick scutter across the kitchen floor and – what amazing luck! The Giant had put on the floor a large piece of toasted bread: just for her and her friends. But the Giant was always generous.

With her two front paws Furball tried shoving the piece of toast. Then she prodded it with her nose. No. Too heavy. So with her sharp teeth she bit off and pouched a good quantity, ran to the dresser, de-pouched, and then ran back to the toast for more. She did this three times. Then she heard oom voices and she skedaddled.

She didn't understand the oom voices, but Kitty was saying, 'I don't know – I don't *know!*'

And Kitty's dad was saying, '*He* can't have gone far.'

'There was just this sudden bang outside the window,' Kitty said. 'A car backfired or something. Radish leaped and I thought he'd just jumped down on the floor.'

'Well, that's probably all he did do.'

'But he's *disappeared.*'

Instinct made Furball run when she heard the ooms yelling. She had only one pouchful of toast but she could come back for the rest when things quietened down. Meanwhile she climbed upwards with two pouches of toast for Mokey and the new Rivals, seven of them. Frankie-boy said he was going to call them Smelly-one, Smelly-two, Smelly-three – and so on up to Smelly-seven. Furball thought this was very unkind but at the same time she found it very amusing. *Fluff. Brick. Dusty tunnel and up against the sooty walls, a wiggle to the left* – instinct-memory took her back towards the fireplace in the living room. And as she came down the final passage, although it was very dark, she was aware of a creature straight ahead of her. A moke? No – something told her it wasn't a moke. There was a smell – but it wasn't a nasty, narky sort of smell. Quite the opposite. It was a delicious smell, a familiar smell. Could it be? Was she just smelling herself? It was a hamster smell!

With her moist little beady-eyes she saw some very similar eyes looking back at her. Hamster eyes. 'Good afternoon,' she said.

The other hamster peered back at her silently. Furball hoped it wasn't a girl-hamster, but, somehow, even in the darkness she could tell that it wasn't.

CHAPTER TWENTY-SIX

In the Piano?

Dad returned to the kitchen.

When Kitty had yelled from upstairs, he'd just made some toast. In his haste to answer, he had dropped the toast from his hand. Now, when he picked it up from the floor, he was puzzled that a large corner of it had been nibbled off.

He went to the broom cupboard and collected the dustpan and brush. He scooped up the remaining crumbs from the floor and looked round the kitchen. Then he picked up the piece of toast again.

If he hadn't been so worried, he might have examined the rows of toothmarks at the corner of his toast. But he was worried. Mum had gone out, and Kitty said she had only looked at her laptop 'for a second' and that Radish had 'just disappeared'.

It was bad enough to have lost their own hamster, Chum, some weeks ago. But to have lost another hamster – Radish – which belonged to someone else…

Dad paced about the kitchen.

Upstairs, in the living room, Kitty was on her hands and knees peering under the chairs and sofa. No Radish. She opened a cupboard and rummaged among some DVDs which she had grown out of years ago, and some board games such as Scrabble which she hardly ever played. When she had searched for Chum in the old days, she had called her name, half believing that the little creature could understand English. Kitty had no such beliefs about Radish. And she knew that her friend Emma didn't care for Radish especially. But Kitty felt responsible for him. Having said she would look after Radish for a few days, she wanted to keep her word. And she dreaded the fuss from her mum and dad if Radish were to go missing. They were sure to say 'I told you so!' – for they'd both been against the idea of looking after Emma's hamster (or *wretched little rat* as

Mum called Radish).

Fussing, as Kitty had known he would, Dad came back. 'Chum got into the piano once – do you remember?' He was still holding the piece of toast on a plate, and put it down by the open fireplace.

'Dad – I don't see how Radish could have got into the piano,' said Kitty. 'I just let him go for a few *seconds*...'

'Hamsters move very fast,' said Dad. He had already gone to the other end of the room where the upright piano was placed against a wall. 'You remember – Chum climbed right down into the works. Lucky none of us play the piano very often or she'd have been beaten to death with the hammers or deafened by the strings.'

'He won't be there, Dad,' said Kitty. But she loyally kneeled down with her dad and helped take the front off the lower part of the piano. As they did it, both of them had their backs to the fireplace.

'Nope,' Kitty said. She was unsurprised.

But dad had now opened the top of the piano and was calling down into the hammers. 'Radish. Ra-a-dish!'

CHAPTER TWENTY-SEVEN

Room Service

'If you waz ter ask me,' said Uncle Sid, 'I'd say it was floor-food.'

'Better than the snapper,' said Frankie-boy perkily, to which Uncle Sid replied, sadly and truthfully, 'You dunno whatcha talkin' of, boy.'

For her part, Mokey Moke – with seven new Rivals to feed, as well as the rest of the family, not to mention Furball and Radish themselves – was very grateful to the hamsters for bringing home such a magnificent, large, buttery piece of toast.

It had been welcome enough when Furball had scurried up and down the chimney three times with her pouches full of chewed toast. But Mokey Moke had never believed the hamster's prattle about the Giant putting the food out specially.

'It's every moke fer issel, Furba,' she'd said. 'Ooms don't *elp* rodents. I keep tellin yer – it's not in their nature.'

'But the Giant,' explained Furball, 'has *always* put food out for me. And now she knows where we are, she will *keep* putting food out.'

Mokey Moke and the others hadn't liked this talk of an oom who knew *where they were*. Some of them spoke in hasty panicky tones of moving on at once before the Giant oom could trap or kill them all. Others dismissed Furball's ideas.

'It's jus *food*,' said Buster. '*Either* it's floor-food – in which case you an *uvver*-amster'd be dead by nar – which you *ain't*. Or it's jus food. It fell on the floor by accident. You got lucky. There ain't no Giant wot puts out toast fer Furball and the mokes.'

'If the Giant knew we were here,' said Furball indignantly, 'she would even save me the trouble of going down the tunnel. She'd bring the toast to this floor.'

'I fought you said she *does* know where you is.'

'She might not know *exactly*,' said Furball cautiously. 'But if she *did*, she'd bring me food.'

'Oh, yeah,' said Buster, 'an put it on a neat little plate for you n all.'

'Perhaps,' said Furball.

It was satisfying to be proved right within a few minutes. While Mokey Moke and others devoured the few pouchfuls of chewed toast which Furball had brought for them, she was able to take Buster to the edge of the brick ledge in the chimney where they were living.

'Love a duck,' said Buster. It was the closest the perky young moke had ever been in his life to admitting he had been wrong.

'Would you help me carry the toast which the Giant has so kindly brought?' Furball inquired. 'On a china plate,' she added, perhaps unnecessarily.

'You betcha!'

But then he froze.

'Supposin.'

Radish, the strong silent type of hamster, who

had not said a word, looked at Buster with particular attention.

'Supposin it's a trick? Supposin the Giant *lets* you nibble off a bit and *then* covers the floor-food with the killer dose. Jus *supposin…*'

But Furball didn't have time for any of this. She scurried down the wall of the chimney, followed by Radish. Between them, the two hamsters were able to push the piece of toast off the plate and carry it back to the shadows of the fireplace. Buster helped them heave it up the sooty wall to their brick ledge.

'Now that,' said Mokey Moke, 'that's what I'd call room service.'

CHAPTER TWENTY-EIGHT

Sherlock Holmes, Otherwise Known as Mum

Kitty's dad didn't mention the toast. He couldn't imagine a mouse being strong enough to carry such a large amount of food. So he concluded it could only have been taken by a rat. And he dreaded the upheaval if Mum thought there were rats hidden in the living room. He looked round in despair. What would she do? Block off the fireplaces? Install a new floor?

In the event, Mum was quite laid back about the disappearance of the visiting hamster. 'Emma never looked after it properly anyway,' she said.

'I know, Mum,' said Kitty. 'But it's one thing for Emma not to look after him, and another for me to *lose* him.'

'They had a guinea-pig – do you remember? It was eaten by an urban fox.'

'That wasn't Emma's fault.'

'Their lizard,' Mum continued, ignoring the plea, 'died of cold when their electricity was cut off.'

'It wasn't *Emma's* fault…'

'And their tropical fish? Do you remember that disaster?'

'Mum, I'd still rather not go to school on Monday morning and say *Sorry, Emma – lost your hamster.*'

Mum looked sharply round the room.

'It disappeared in seconds, you say.'

'Honestly, Mum – one second. Radish was beside me on the sofa. The next, he'd just *vanished.*'

'Then there's only one explanation,' said Mum. 'Sherlock Holmes: *when you have eliminated the impossible, whatever remains, however improbable, must be the truth.*'

'So,' asked Dad, 'where *is* he?'

'He *could* have run out on to the landing,' said Mum, 'but then one of you would have seen him. He *could* have climbed into the piano, but he isn't there – you've searched it. And you've looked under all the furniture and in the cupboard. So he must be hiding up the chimney.'

She lay down near the opening of the fireplace and peered up into the blackness. 'I can't see him, but I'm sure he's up there somewhere. If you put a dish of food down beside the hearthstone and a little dish of water, he'll come when he's hungry.'

CHAPTER TWENTY-NINE

A Wonderfully Soft Sock

The noise made by the ooms at the entrance to the moke's cave, and the thrusting of an oom head into the chimney, within inches of their brick ledge, flung the mokes and hamsters into confusion.

'Didn't I always say?' asked Uncle Sid, 'Didn't I *always* say it was madness coming up ere? Madness.'

No one gave a direct answer since no one wanted to be rude to Uncle Sid. The truthful reply would have been *no*. He had never said it was madness to run up the chimney. He had scuttled up here, almost by accident, just like everyone else. But having got there, it was obviously sensible to ask themselves if it was safe to stay.

'The ooms isn't going ter stick their eds up chimblee every flippin minute,' said Mokey Moke.

And yet while this was true, there were others who believed the ooms were too close for comfort.

'I knew that food on a plate was too good to be true,' said Buster.

'Didn't I always say?' asked Uncle Sid. 'I didn't go an say it *must* be floor-food, but didn't I say – it's a trap, a low-darn oom trap.'

While the mokes discussed their position, Radish nudged Furball into the further recesses of the dark chimney, and the two hamsters went exploring together. They climbed up one floor of the house and found themselves, though Furball didn't realise this at first, in another fireplace. From the living room fireplace they had climbed only a few metres and now found themselves in Kitty's bedroom. As soon as they came cautiously out into the room, Furball sensed that it was familiar. It felt like coming home.

There was the Giant's bed where Furball – or Chum – liked to rummage among the toys and blankets. There was the row of books where she liked to hide. There was her old house, on the floor by the window – the house which Nobby had so contemptuously called *stir*, but which had always been so cosy and comfortable.

Radish didn't say anything, but he ran across the carpet and in through the open door of the cage. There was still some water left in Chum's old water-bottle. And it was *Chum's* water-bottle, not Furball's – it seemed important to think of herself by her old name now.

Radish was drinking eagerly.

'Leave some for me,' she squeaked.

His habit of not speaking, his absolute *non-communication*, was something, at the moment, which she liked very much indeed. He looked at her through the bars of the cage in a *meaningful* sort of a way, and he said nothing. She stepped into the cage gingerly.

It was good to be able to drink. She did so thirstily for some minutes and felt much refreshed. Then she scampered out of the cage. Although he was not *saying* anything, she knew what Radish was thinking. He was thinking: *this is a hamster cage. We've got straw here, water, seeds, an upstairs for fooling about in, a downstairs, plastic tubes for scuttling in and a wonderfully soft sock as a bed. Why would we want to leave this behind, now we have found it? Why leave this for a dark, dangerous, sooty hole up a chimney to live with a lot of mokes?*

Chum – for she would always be Chum to the ooms who didn't even know about her life as Furball – asked *herself* these difficult questions, but she knew she couldn't just *abandon* the mokes.

She wanted to tell Radish that she had experienced a number of wonderful things with the mokes which she had never known to be possible while she was just living in the cage and being the Giant's *pet* (that word that Buster and Nobby had said with such scorn). She wanted to tell Radish that she had been in terrible danger and known awful fear, but it had been worth it. She didn't use the word *freedom*, but she had been able to scurry anywhere and that made life a thousand times better than it could ever be in a cage – even if she was in a cage with another, very nice, silent male hamster like Radish. And the other thing was, she'd made friends with the mokes themselves and she wasn't sure that was something she wanted to give up – tempted though she was by the safe world of the cage with its regular seeds

and water and treats.

'Nice to have a bit of a wash, eh?' she said as Radish licked his small pink paws and rubbed them against his face.

He looked back at her as though he agreed, but he didn't actually say anything.

'Here,' she said, moving towards him. She licked her own paw and wiped a bit of soot off his forehead.

Some time later, she decided it was time to go back down to the mokes. Radish didn't appear happy about this, but he followed her all the same.

And, some time even later than that (hamster time

is different from human time, remember), Chum persuaded the mokes to come and build a nest in the chimney of Kitty's bedroom.

There were many objections. Uncle Sid, quite reasonably, pointed out that it was two floors up from the larder and the kitchen. To this, it was answered that the Giant quite often had snacks in her room, so they could help themselves to apple cores, biscuits and such.

'You can't *live* on apple cores and such,' said Uncle Sid.

But as Mokey Moke told him, it depended how many mokes there were. Some of them scampered off, never to be seen again. Moke life was like that. Mokes are not sentimental. Mokey Moke didn't seem bothered by their vanishing.

'I knows why you want us up in the bedroom, Furball – course I does,' she said.

'Oh?'

Chum didn't really know herself. It just *felt* right.

'You always want to *settle* a bit at this stage,' said Mokey Moke mysteriously.

Chum had no idea what the little moke meant. Mokey Moke nodded, and smiled, and rolled her eyes – *know what I mean* – no need to spell things out among friends.

'Don't leave us just yet – eh?' said Mokey Moke. 'Think about it – eh?'

'I don't want to leave you,' said Chum, who was upset by her friend's words. 'Of course I don't.'

'I know we can't offer the comfort what yer get in stir,' said Mokey Moke. 'But that don't stop it *being* stir all the same. Like it or lump it, you're *locked in*. Yer can't get out, can yer – not in stir. And then – well, yer in *their* ands, arencha?'

Chum wanted to say that it was *nice* being in the Giant's hands. She felt safe with the Giant. Why couldn't she go back to the Giant and sleep in the sock *and* go on being friends with Mokey Moke and the others.

'Cos,' said Mokey Moke mysteriously. 'Cos. Just cos. I'm not saying what Buster and Nobby said bout ole Murph was right. I'm not saying vat, am I?'

'Of course not, Mokey Moke,' said Chum, feeling a little confused.

'I didn't see them ooms put im in gardin and fer all I know they means yer no arm. All I know is – oh, I'm a moke. Yer wouldn't get me locked up in stir even though they does give yer – what was it they give yer ter sleep in?'

'A sock,' said Chum with a sad little sigh, remembering how very soft, and how very cosy that sock was, and how delicious her sleeps were in it.

'Course – Buster – Sid – well, they're male, aren't they?'

'So it seems, Mokey Moke.'

'So, course, they're never gonna understand how yer feel, girlie – not like I do. Like I say – when I'm up the duff I looks round for a nest. A bit of stability, like. Course, I know ow you feels. It's just – well, it is stir. They do lock you in. What does *e* feel about it all?'

Chum was even more confused by now. What was Mokey Moke saying? By *e*, she must mean Radish. What Radish felt about anything was a complete mystery. What he felt about *it all* was impossible to say. What was *it all*?

'Only,' said Mokey Moke, 'with you being in an

interesting condition, you'll be looking for somewhere comfortable. I do me-sell. Looks rahnd for an extra soft bit of fluff, like, or somewhere I can be safe, quiet like.'

'Really?' asked Chum. She wasn't aware of being in any condition and wondered why Mokey Moke should have said she was *interesting*.

When the other mokes heard that her condition was *interesting*, they all clustered round and made remarks which she didn't understand.

'You didn't waste much time, didja?' was Uncle Sid's quite friendly observation. He even managed a chuckle with it.

Buster was just coming into the new nest. He was dragging a bit of carrot. 'Don't fink it's floor-food,' he gasped. 'Found it down there by the cave entrance. Oo don't waste time?'

'Furball,' chuckled Uncle Sid.

'Oh, yeah,' said Buster. 'I eard. Congratulations, Furball. You're a dark horse.'

'Oh, no,' said Chum politely, 'simply a brown hamster.' And they all laughed more than ever.

CHAPTER THIRTY

Home at Last

Sherlock Holmes, otherwise known as Mum, concluded that Radish was still up the chimney somewhere. 'He took the bit of carrot I put out for him,' she argued. 'Who else do you think took it? Father Christmas?'

Kitty and Dad agreed that it was a good sign, though Kitty noticed Dad had gone a bit quiet when asked *who else* might be living up the chimney.

They were all together in the living room watching TV. Tomorrow was another school day, and they agreed that they shouldn't go to bed too late. Still, there was the usual struggle – Dad telling Kitty to go to bed, and Kitty saying she would go but not yet – and eventually her agreeing to go upstairs to put on her pyjamas and clean her teeth.

Kitty's mum and dad sat downstairs together.

'We'll give it a day or two more,' said Mum. 'Then we'll have to give up poor little Radish for lost.'

'We don't have a very good record with hamsters,' agreed Dad.

'I think,' said Mum, 'that I'm just going to throw the cage away. That catch on the door was broken – which was how Chum escaped in the first place.'

Both of them sighed and drank some wine. But the peace didn't last long.

'Mum! Dad!' Kitty was calling down the stairs.

'Come quickly. You'll never guess who's in the hamster's cage! It's not just Radish – it's Chum! And, Mum, she looks really well – it's almost like she's got *fatter*. Oh, Mum – do come!'

Keep reading for

GAMES

PUZZLES

and

THINGS TO MAKE AND DO

MISTER PETER'S PUZZLE

Can you find all these
words in the wordsearch?

Can you remember what
all the words mean?

furball	kitty	mouse
moke	hamster	cage
nobby	chum	sandwich
seeds	fevvas	narks

```
y m o u s e b k v c
e o n x g q t h f n
y d k i t t y a u o
t f m y c h u m r b
k i o n a r k s b b
a m k l f y e t a y
y f e v v a s e l c
s e e d s o c r l a
n k m s r j s l i g
s a n d w i c h x e
```

MOKEY MOKE'S
MOUSEY MAZE

Mokey Moke is hungry!

Can you draw a path to
help her get to the bread?

The Giant's
Join-the-Dots

Furball's lost her fur!

Can you join the dots and
make her fluffy again?

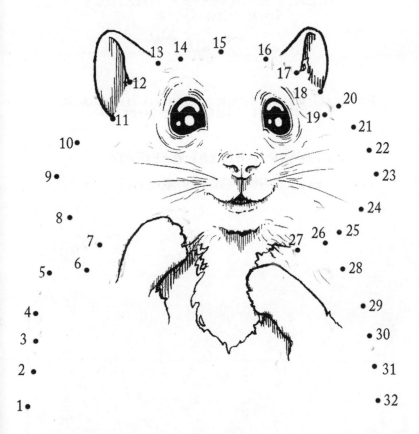

FURBALL'S HAMSTER HIDEOUT

Furball loves snuggling in her sock.

**Make your pet a comfy
place to sleep.**

You will need:

An empty plastic ice cream tub
Scissors
Shredded newspaper
An old, clean sock

1.   Clean and dry your ice cream tub, and throw away the lid.

2.   Ask a grown-up to cut a hole out of one side, to make a doorway.

3.   Turn the tub upside down and place it in the cage, like a mini house.

4.   Fill your hamster house with shredded newspaper, and a comfortable old sock.

THE SNARK SUPER SWING

Snarks are what ooms call squirrels, and
they love jumping around in the trees.

Give your pet a mini-playground
so he or she can get active too!

You will need:

A cardboard tube a bit longer than your hamster
Scissors or a compass
A piece of string twice the height of your cage

1. Ask a grown-up to cut the tube in half, long-ways. Choose the bigger half to use for your swing, and then poke a small hole through either end.

2. Thread the piece of string down through one hole, along the underside of the cardboard, and pull it up through the hole at the other end.

4. Put the swing in the cage, and ask a grown-up to help you tie the two long ends of the string securely to the roof of the cage.

5. Make sure the swing is close to the floor so your hamster can get in and out easily.

KITTY'S KITCHEN TREATS

Kitty loves to make sure her
pet is always pampered.

Here are some delicious dinners
you can make at home for hamsters,
gerbils and mice.

FRUITY CEREAL ROLLS

You will need:

Half a banana
A teaspoon of crushed cornflakes
Finely chopped apple
A small handful of oats

1.   Mash up the banana, cornflakes and oats until the mixture looks smooth.

2.   Mix in the finely chopped apple.

3.   Roll the mixture into balls, small enough that your hamster can hold them easily.

4.   Let the fruit rolls harden slightly in the fridge before feeding them to your pet.

PEANUT BUTTER PIZZA

You will need:

A thin slice of brown bread
A teaspoon of peanut butter
Grated carrot (or grated celery)
Sunflower seeds

1. Cut a circle out of the bread using an upside-down mug.

2. Spread the peanut butter on the circle of bread.

3. Sprinkle grated carrot over the top.

4. Arrange the sunflower seeds on top.

5. Cut it in quarters to look like pizza slices.

BANANA AND BLUEBERRY PUDDING

You will need:

Half a banana
Half a teaspoon of honey
Sunflower seeds
Raisins

1.   Mash up the banana and honey.

2.   Add some sunflower seeds and raisins.

3.   Mix again, so it's nice and gooey.

4.   Serve it in your pet's food bowl.